"You didn't really think he'd stop seeing me, did you?"

"Yes," Minta answered slowly.

"And you believed him?" Delia's voice sounded bitter.

Minta gathered her courage to ask the all-important question. "Your letter said that I'd be dispensable after my baby was born. What—what did you mean?"

Delia stared at her for a long moment. "Why do you think Dane married you when he had me? He wanted to make you pregnant—to make sure of your father's money.

"I don't believe it," Minta moaned. "I can't believe it!"

"He comes here often. He laughs about you, about the way you threw yourself at him in London, about your clumsiness in bed...."

Minta's heart wrestled with her mind in an anguish of uncertainty as Delia's outline began to blur and swim in front of her eyes.

Books by Sally Wentworth

HARLEQUIN PRESENTS

HARLEQUIN ROMANCES

These books may be available at your local bookseller.

For a list of all titles currently available,
send your name and address to:

Harlequin Reader Service
P.O. Box 52040, Phoenix, AZ 85072-2040
Canadian address: P.O. Box 2800, Postal Station A,
5170 Yonge St., Willowdale, Ont. M2N 5T5

SALLY WENTWORTH

dark awakening

Harlequin Books

TORONTO • NEW YORK • LONDON
AMSTERDAM • PARIS • SYDNEY • HAMBURG
STOCKHOLM • ATHENS • TOKYO • MILAN

Harlequin Presents first edition October 1984
ISBN 0-373-10733-1

Original hardcover edition published in 1984
by Mills & Boon Limited

CHAPTER ONE

THE phone rang just as Minta was leaving the house. For a moment she toyed with not bothering to answer it, but then turned and ran into the sitting-room to pick up the receiver, its bleep too insistent to ignore. 'Hallo?'

'Minta, I've invited someone back for dinner tonight.'

'Oh, Dad, no! I've got a date tonight. Can't you take him out somewhere?'

'Sorry, darling, it's too late; I've already arranged for him to come to the house at seven-thirty.'

'Oh, lor! Another one of your crusty old customers, I suppose?'

Her father, who was by no means old himself, sounded amused. 'I wouldn't call him crusty exactly.'

Minta sighed but said submissively, 'Okay, I'll put my date back a couple of hours. And I suppose I'd better phone Maggie to come and make the numbers up.'

'Fine,' Richard Tennant agreed. 'I was going to suggest it myself.'

'You should watch it,' Minta told him teasingly. 'If you introduce your girl-friend to all your rich customers you'll be in danger of losing her!'

He chuckled. 'I don't think there's much chance of that happening with the man I'm bringing tonight.'

Minta groaned. 'He must be about ninety, then. What's his name?'

'Dane Fenton. You won't have heard of him before, he lives abroad most of the time.'

'A pity he didn't stay there,' Minta muttered under her breath.

She said goodbye and then made two more phone calls; one to Maggie, a sophisticated and highly successful career-girl, who admitted to being in her mid-thirties, who had her own business and was the latest of her father's many girl-friends. And the other to her own boy-friend, who wasn't very happy about being put off for a dinner guest of her father's.

'It's only for a couple of hours,' Minta said placatingly. 'I'll meet you there round about ten.'

After some grumbling he agreed, and she was free to go out, but now her shopping included a trip to the supermarket to buy provisions for this evening's meal. Minta and her father, a merchant banker, lived in a tall Georgian house in a terrace in one of the more exclusive squares near Mayfair. Since his wife's death, over ten years ago, Richard Tennant had employed a very efficient housekeeper, but Minta had taken a Cordon Bleu cookery course and now cooked dinner more often than not.

She got home before five and immediately set about preparing the meal, nothing too elaborate, and basically English dishes as their guest was a foreigner. At six-thirty she had got as far as she could and went up to bath and change. Bearing in mind that she was going on to a rock club after dinner, Minta put on a pair of soft black velvet evening trousers and a cream blouse with deep ruffles at the neck, which would just have to do for both. Her thick fair hair she brushed into its usual shining, shoulder-length style, and then she did her face, adding green shadow to emphasise her hazel eyes. She was of average height, which she didn't like, so always wore high heels to make her look taller, tonight putting on a pair of black patent slingbacks.

While she was getting ready, her father came home and called a greeting as he passed her door, then she heard him whistling and singing in the shower, and smiled to herself, glad of his happiness when she remembered the long months after her mother's death when he had been so silent and closed-in within himself. As soon as she was ready, Minta ran down to the kitchen to check on the meal and put the last-minute touches to the dining table. Richard Tennant soon joined her, looking maturely handsome in a wine velvet jacket and bow tie.

Minta pretended to be disapproving. 'If you're not careful one of your girl-friends is going to snap you up and marry you!'

He grinned as he put some wine in the fridge to chill. 'I'm not sure, but I think there was a compliment in there somewhere! You don't have to worry, I'm quite safe with Maggie; she likes her independence as much as I do.'

Minta looked at him speculatively, wondering if he was right—he'd been seeing Maggie for over six months now and she might well become a habit to have around, and also Minta had noticed that Maggie had started to leave some of her things here: a couple of sexy nighties and a change of clothes for when she stayed the night. Maybe this was the first step to establishing a permanent claim. Impulsively she said, 'If I weren't here, would you have Maggie move in?'

He lifted a quizzical eyebrow. 'Are you thinking of leaving?'

'No, of course not.'

'Then the question doesn't arise, does it?' But he saw

the doubt in her eyes and came over to put his hands on her shoulders. 'My dear child, I'm perfectly happy as I am. No one can take your mother's place, you know that. Maggie's fun and we're fond of each other, but we're certainly not committed to the relationship. So don't go getting any crazy ideas about leaving me a clear field. I need you around. Who else can I get to charm unwilling customers into seeing reason? And besides,' he added as an afterthought, 'Maggie can't cook anywhere near as well as you do.'

She laughed. 'Now that I believe, but my reputation as a cook will be ruined if you don't get out of the way so that I can put the vegetables on!' But there was relief in her eyes as she moved away. Minta loved her father unreservedly and felt no jealousy of his women. He had been only thirty-nine when her mother died and he had grieved for her sincerely, probably still did, but he was young and vigorous; he couldn't live like a monk and she didn't expect him to. But if he had shown any signs of wanting to marry again and was holding back because of her, then Minta would have moved out, willing to be a little lonely and unhappy herself because she loved him too much ever to become an obstacle to his happiness.

They kept a special bottle of sherry in a cupboard, and her father went to this and poured out two glasses, bringing one across to her. It was a little habit they had formed, this quiet drink together before their guests arrived. They were both gregarious people and had many friends, so often had dinner guests or were invited out in their turn, which made this quarter of an hour a special time for shared confidences, for advice and for future plans.

'What are we having for dinner?' Richard Tennant

asked, lifting the lid of one of the saucepans. 'Smells good.'

'Wait and see. You think of nothing but your stomach,' Minta admonished him.

Richard Tennant grinned amiably. He began to tell her about his day at the bank, just the general outline; he never discussed the details of his clients' private business with her. 'I was supposed to be having lunch with Fenton, but his plane was delayed and he didn't turn up until three; that's why I asked him to dinner,' he told her.

'Where does he come from?' Minta asked absently as she concentrated on stirring the gravy.

'The Canary Islands. He has Spanish connections.' He was about to tell her more, but just then the front door bell rang. 'Perhaps that's him now, I'll go.'

But it was Maggie, exactly on time for once. She swept into the kitchen in a stunning blue satin dress on a wave of Chanel that almost drowned the cooking smells. 'Hallo, Minta darling. You're looking marvellous. How are things?' She aimed a kiss in the general direction of her cheek and then sat on one of the pine kitchen stools and accepted the glass of sherry that Richard Tennant handed to her. Without waiting for Minta to answer, she turned to him and began to tell him a funny story about something that had happened to her earlier that day. She had a droll way with words and told the story well, holding his attention and making him laugh in genuine enjoyment. Minta stood by the stove and watched them while she stirred her gravy with one hand and sipped her sherry with the other. Maggie was taller and thinner than herself, with shining red hair that owed much to her hairdresser's skill with the tint bottle, and her features were good with few signs yet of ageing. And she had a vivacious personality that made most people like her at once. As Minta watched her she felt a prick of jealousy for her sophistication and a slight resentment for the way she had come down to the kitchen to join them, as if she was a member of the family, instead of being entertained upstairs as a guest. But then she pushed the thought aside; after all, they had known Maggie long enough now to be on informal terms.

Five minutes later the bell rang again and her father took Maggie with him as he went upstairs to answer it, leaving Minta free to quickly and expertly do as much as she could in the preparation of the meal and leave it safely simmering. Then she in turn went up to greet their guest, hoping that he wasn't a vegetarian or so old that he didn't have any teeth left.

Fully expecting to meet some greybeard, she pushed open the door to the drawing room—and stopped in surprise when she saw her father talking to a tall, dark-haired man who, although he had his back to her, had far too athletic a figure to be old or even elderly. The three of them were standing in front of her father's proudest possession, a Turner seascape, which hung over the marble fireplace, and Minta should have guessed from the attention Maggie was paying him that their guest was also good-looking. Maggie liked good-looking men and she liked even more to be seen with them.

Her father saw her first and turned, a grin on his face at her surprise. 'Ah, there you are. Dane, I'd like you to meet my daughter, Araminta. This is Dane Fenton.'

The man turned to meet her and Minta automatically held out her hand. He was younger, even, than she had thought, only about thirty, very tanned, with thick dark hair that had a definite curl and pale grey eyes that were looking at her with as much surprise in them as in her own.

'How do you do, Miss Tennant?' He took her hand in a grip that was strong but didn't hurt, as some men's did who felt the need to exert their personalities. 'I hope my coming here at the last minute hasn't been too much trouble for you?'

Minta disclaimed, again surprised by his voice, which had a deep, rich timbre and was impeccably English, whereas she had expected at the least a foreign accent. She gave her father a quick, accusing glance and he grinned, glad that his little joke had come off.

'Cooking is never too much trouble for Minta,' he said, coming to put a proud arm round her waist. 'She's a fully-trained Cordon Bleu cook. I can guarantee you'll enjoy her food just as much as any at a first class restaurant.'

'Daddy, really! Now what do I do if the whole meal is a complete disaster?'

'I'm sure it will be delicious,' Dane said gallantly.

Minta smiled at him. 'You'd better try it first.'

Maggie, impatient at being ignored, broke in. 'Richard said you lived in the Canary Islands, but he didn't say which one.'

'Mostly in Gran Canaria, at Las Palmas, but I also have an office in Tenerife and spend a lot of my time there.'

'Oh, really. What do you do?'

A slightly closed look came into his face. 'Property development,' he answered shortly, then turned to his host. 'You hadn't finished telling me how you found your Turner.'

Richard Tennant needed no prompting to finish his

favourite story, and then they all talked about pictures
in general until Minta stood up and suggested they go
in to dinner. She had prepared a basically simple menu
of soup, rolled cod with a wine sauce, boeuf en croûte
with vegetables, then a good variety of English cheeses,
and finally a selection of three puddings: sherry trifle, a
charlotte russe and a lemon sorbet. Although her
carefully chosen English meal seemed somewhat wasted
now that it was obvious that Dane Fenton was as
English as they were.

But he was very appreciative, praising every dish just
enough for it not to sound like fulsome flattery. He also
kept up his end of the conversation, showing an alert
and intelligent mind and a comprehensive grasp of
contemporary affairs even though he lived so far from
the centre of things. She and her father were sitting at
each end of the table, their guests between them, the
table closed down to a size where they were near
enough to talk intimately in twos or generally among
the four of them. And there was much laughter, all of
them enjoying themselves, and the wine they drank
helping to break down any barriers. Maggie sparkled,
at her best in this sort of atmosphere, casually flirting a
little with both men, but devoting most of her time to
Richard Tennant, which left Dane free to talk to Minta,
and he seemed to want to know all about her.

'Do you cook professionally?' he asked, after she had
brought in the coffee and they sat drinking it alongside
balloons of brandy.

'Occasionally. For the last couple of years, whenever
my father holds an official board meeting at the bank I
cook lunch for all the directors. And now word has
spread a little and I quite often get asked to cook for
similar functions at other businesses.'

'You wouldn't like to work in a hotel or something, as a chef?'

Minta shook her head. 'Daddy wouldn't be very keen on my doing that; he likes me to be here to cook for him.' She smiled at him, liking his clean-cut features and the way one of his dark brows rose slightly above the other when he asked a question.

'And do you look after this place all by yourself?'

'Oh, no. We have a very good housekeeper; I just do the cooking and she takes care of everything else.'

'And are there just the two of you, or do you have brothers and sisters?'

'No, I'm the only one. How about you—do you have any family?' Minta asked as she poured out more coffee.

Again a closed look seemed to come into his face. 'I have an elder half-brother, that's all.' Then he changed the subject rather abruptly, Minta thought, turning to ask her father a question so that conversation became general again for a while until Dane drew Minta out to talk about her other interests.

It was almost eleven when the phone rang. Minta had been so absorbed in talking to Dane that she had completely forgotten the time, but now she glanced at her watch and gave an exclamation of dismay. 'Oh, my God, that must be Gerald!' Quickly she excused herself and ran to answer it.

'I know what you're going to say and I'm sorry,' she said before her angry boy-friend had time to say a word. 'I just forgot the time.'

'I've been standing here propping up the wall for over an hour,' Gerald informed her heatedly. 'There are plenty of other girls around if you can't be bothered to get here, you know.'

Minta with difficulty stifled an impulse to tell him to find himself one, then, but after all, he did have some reason to be angry. 'I've said I'm sorry,' she pointed out. 'What do you want me to do—crawl?'

'No, just get yourself over here—fast.'

Minta suddenly knew that she didn't want to go. 'It is late, Gerald. There hardly seems much point in . . .'

But he wasn't going to stand for that. 'This place stays open till two, and you can be here in twenty minutes.'

She sighed in reluctant assent. It occurred to her for the first time that she really would have to do something about Gerald, he was getting to be a bore, even if he was an Honourable and extremely eligible, a fact of which he was only too well aware. 'Oh, all right; I'll be there as soon as I can.'

Going back into the dining-room, she came up behind her father and put her hands on his shoulders. 'Sorry, Daddy, I shall have to go. I've already kept Gerald waiting for an age.'

Richard Tennant patted her hand indulgently. 'All right, I understand.' Gerald's father was one of his co-directors at the bank and he, too, thought him a good match for her. 'I'm sure Dane will excuse you.'

The younger man stood up. 'You're going out? Perhaps I can give you a lift; I have a car outside.'

'Nonsense, you mustn't rush off just because Minta has a date. Stay and have another brandy,' her father protested.

But Dane Fenton declined firmly. 'Thank you, you're very kind, but it's really time I was leaving. It was an excellent meal and I enjoyed it immensely; so much that the least I can do is offer Minta a lift.' He smiled at her, his eyes warm, so that she found herself smiling in return.

'Thank you; it will save me phoning for a taxi. I'll get my coat.'

The chill of the November night caught her as Minta waited for Dane to say his goodbyes to Maggie and her father, then the door shut behind him and he came to quickly escort her a few yards down the street to a car parked at the kerb. He helped her in and then went round the other side to the driver's seat. 'Where to?'

'De Sade's Cellar. It's a rock club near Covent Garden.'

His mouth twisted with amusement at the name. 'I know the general area, but then you'll have to direct me.'

For a few minutes Minta felt rather tonguetied, which was quite unlike her, but alone with him in the car she was very much aware of Dane Fenton, of his strangeness and his masculinity. He was very self-confident, of course, but then most of the young men she knew were; because they came from backgrounds where money and the privilege it brought had always been there from birth. But Dane had much more than that; he had excellent manners coupled with an easy charm that made him immediately likeable, and these, together with his good looks, made a heady combination. Although he was young to be a business associate of her father's, he was at least five years older than the young men she was used to going around with, and it showed in the way he handled himself, speaking to her father as an equal, not as someone in a different generation. And it showed, too, in the way he discussed worldly topics with reasoned out arguments and not set opinions. Also, Minta somehow had the feeling that he would be good at handling women, that in that, too, he would have wide experience.

'Is this your car?' she asked him, for something to say.

'No, I hired it at the airport. I prefer to drive myself rather than depend on taxis all the time.' He paused to concentrate on overtaking a bus. 'I take it this Gerald is your boy-friend?'

'Yes.'

'Is it serious?' he asked casually.

'No,' Minta denied emphatically, although up until tonight she had thought that she could be quite willing to be serious about Gerald. 'I've just known him for a long time, that's all.'

'I see.' He turned to flash a smile at her. 'You'll have to be careful; those are the most dangerous kinds of relationships—the ones that you just drift into.'

His smile really turned her on; Minta felt a thrill of pleasure run through her veins and set out to make him smile again by telling him of a funny incident when Maggie's cat, Fred, had got stuck on a ledge outside her fourth-storey flat and she had called the fire brigade in a panic, forgetting to tell them that it was only a cat on the ledge. They had turned up with sirens blaring, accompanied by an ambulance and several police cars, and just as they all arrived, the cat walked in the window. Maggie had been so appalled that she'd hidden in the flat and not dared come out for hours.

Dane laughed with genuine amusement. 'Is Maggie staying with you and your father?'

'No, she has her own flat in Chelsea. She runs her own business and is terribly clever.'

Perhaps something showed in her voice, because Dane gave her a quick glance. 'Are she and your father engaged?'

'No.' Minta shook her head and confided, 'He's had

quite a few girl-friends since Mummy died; Maggie's just the latest.'

Again he looked amused. 'You seem very blasé about it. How long do they usually last?'

She shrugged. 'It varies. Some just a few weeks, others for almost a year. He's been going with Maggie for more than six months now.'

'And no signs of wanting to make it permanent?'

'He says not. Because of Mummy, you see; he always says that no one can take her place. Oh, you turn right here, by the way,' she added as they drove past the portico of the old Covent Garden market which had now been turned into shops and restaurants. She gave him some directions until he pulled up opposite the neon flashing sign saying 'De Sade's Cellar'.

'Is this one of your "in" places?' asked Dane, looking at the sign with a slight frown.

'I suppose so. A lot of the top groups get here.' Even from where they were sitting in the car they could hear the throb of sound coming through the narrow doorway; it almost made the car shake. 'And you can wear what you like, nobody cares. Some people look really weird.'

'I can imagine,' he remarked drily, then turned to her. 'I haven't been in a place like that for years. Would you mind if I came in with you to see what it's like?'

Minta's eyes ran over his well-cut evening suit. 'Er—I don't quite know how to say this, but you'll look a little out of place.'

Dane grinned. 'Maybe I'll start a new fashion by wearing an old one.'

But Minta still looked doubtful. 'People can get nasty sometimes. If they think you're making fun of them, they might . . .' Her voice trailed off.

'Don't worry,' Dane said gently. 'I can take care of myself, you know.'

And it was then that Minta recognised another quality in him that she had only sensed before; the touch of steel behind his charm.

The lights in the Cellar were dim and it took a few minutes for their eyes to get used to it. The room was packed solid with people, and they stood by the steps, close by where the manager, in a blue, chocolate soldier's uniform, was keeping an eye on the place. On the stage a group of girl musicians, their clothes almost as weird as their hair and make-up, were playing their instruments as if there was no tomorrow, putting everything they had into it as they threw themselves wildly about the stage.

'They gave this place the wrong name,' Dane murmured in her ear as he looked down on the grotesquely dressed, writhing dancers, the coloured lights that swept over them adding to the macabre scene. 'They should have called it Hell's Kitchen.'

Minta hadn't looked at the place like that before, she'd always just walked in and become a part of it, but now she did see that it was like some old pictures of Hell. She was about to agree with him when someone caught her arm.

'So you're here at last!' Gerald, his eyes more accustomed to the darkness, was standing below her, an exasperated frown on his face.

He went to pull her down into the room, but Minta hung back. 'Gerald, this is Dane Fenton.'

He looked up in surprise, which deepened when his eyes went over Dane's clothes. He himself was wearing riding boots and breeches with a black and gold shirt and several neck chains. 'What's he doing here?' he demanded with only a token attempt to lower his voice.

'I was curious to see the place,' Dane informed him casually, adding with a steady look, 'Do you mind?'

Gerald obviously did, but he wilted under Dane's eyes. 'No,' he mumbled, then determinedly pulled Minta on to the floor. 'Let's dance.'

Immediately the noise of the music closed over them as they were swallowed up among the gyrating dancers. It was terribly noisy; the sound beat against their ears like something solid. Minta looked up at Dane leaning against the wall watching them, but then they were pushed further into the throng and she couldn't see him any more.

'What the hell did you want to bring him along for?' Gerald demanded angrily.

'I told you; he gave me a lift and wanted to come in and see what it's like here. I don't suppose he'll stay long.'

'I should hope not. A great evening this is turning out to be,' Gerald observed sulkily. 'Get rid of him; we don't want him around.'

It was obvious that he wanted to be placated, for her to apologise profusely again and give him all her attention. Ordinarily Minta probably would have done; she didn't like people to be annoyed with her, and even less did she like scenes, especially in public, but her eyes went to the doorway again and she saw Dane with a glass in his hand, which he raised to her in silent toast, and suddenly she grew impatient with Gerald. 'Oh, for heaven's sake,' she snapped, raising her voice to be heard above the noise, 'I was late and I've apologised. If you're going to sulk like a schoolboy about it all night, then I'm leaving!'

Which was so unlike her that Gerald gaped at her in amazement. Minta went to move away, and he hastily caught hold of her arm. 'Don't be silly. I'm not sulking. You can't expect me to like you turning up with another man in tow, now can you?' He started dancing again so that Minta had to join in. 'I wanted you all to myself,' he told her, and smiled at her, turning on the charm so obviously that it was blatant.

Minta looked at him with raised eyebrows. Going off at him like that appeared to have worked wonders; maybe he wasn't used to having his ego pricked by one of his girl-friends. They went on dancing in silence, not touching, just moving to the thudding beat of the music. On the stage the female group were going wild, the singer doing impossible things with the hand-mike that made the men near the stage stop dancing to watch while they howled for more. At last the girl reached the climax of the song and then threw herself exhausted on to the stage, her face bathed in perspiration.

Gerald tried to keep her by him on the dance floor, but Minta shook her head. 'No, we must find Dane.'

He was still where they'd left him and he had drinks for them both, which was a miracle at De Sade's.

'Scotch all right for you?' he asked Gerald as he passed over the glass. 'And I got something longer for you,' he said to Minta, handing her a glass of interesting-looking pale green liquid.

'Mmm, lovely. How on earth did you manage to fight your way to the bar? It's always so hot and crowded here that you just can't get a drink unless you queue for at least half an hour.'

Dane shrugged. 'I just told the manager what drinks I wanted and he sent someone to fetch them.'

Gerald gave a small laugh. 'I'll have to try that next time!'

Experimentally taking a sip of her drink, Minta found it to her liking. 'What is it?' she asked Dane.

'Vodka and lime. Okay?'

'Yes, fine.' She felt rather flattered that he'd got her something out of the ordinary.

The music started again and Gerald finished his drink at a gulp. He put a possessive hand on Minta's arm. 'Come on, let's dance.'

'In a minute.' She shook him off and turned to Dane, a mischievous look in her hazel eyes. 'What do you think of the place?' He raised his eyebrows and she repeated the question above the noise.

He leant forward, putting a casual hand on her waist, and spoke into her ear so that she could hear. 'I can think of lots of places you'd enjoy more.'

Minta smiled. 'I didn't think it would be your scene.'

'Why don't you let me take you on to somewhere I know you'd like?'

She looked at him in surprise. He had made the suggestion quite casually, but there was a distinct challenge in his slightly mocking smile, as if he was daring her to accept. It excited her, made her heart beat a little faster. 'What about Gerald?' she mouthed, turning away from the younger man who stood impatiently by, attempting not to look as if he was trying to listen.

Dane's left eyebrow rose. 'He would come too, of course.'

'I don't know. I . . .'

But Gerald interrupted her by saying to Dane. 'I expect you're bored, old boy. Don't think you have to stay here to see Minta home, I'll take care of her.' Then he determinedly made her dance with him again.

But Dane didn't take the hint, he was still there when

the music ended, and Minta insisted on rejoining him. He looked at her steadily when she came up, the mocking challenge plain in his eyes.

Minta found it quite irresistible. Impulsively she turned to Gerald and said, 'This place is just too crowded and noisy. And it's getting boring. Let's go on somewhere else.'

He was inclined to be indignant, having discovered De Sade's himself. 'You've always liked it before.'

'Well, now I don't,' Minta told him impatiently. 'It's always the same here.' He argued for several minutes until she said, 'Okay, if you like it so much, then you stay, but Dane and I are going.' So then Gerald had no choice but to leave with them.

Dane had taken no part in the argument but gave her a glance of approval that made her feel warm all over as they left. He led the way towards his car, but Gerald hung back.

'I've got my own car here. Minta can come with me and you can follow us. I know several places we can go on to.'

But Dane had already unlocked his car door and was holding it open for her. Without a second's hesitation Minta walked across and got in. 'Dane knows of a good place. You can follow us,' she said to Gerald. He didn't think much of that, but grimly went to collect his car, hooting imperiously to let them know when he came up behind them.

This time Dane knew the way and didn't have to ask for directions. It was after midnight and the streets were emptier and darker now, all the theatre and cinema audiences having gone home, and most of the shops having turned out the lights in their windows. There were only private cars, a few late buses and some taxis cruising round looking for a fare. Dane drove efficiently, not taking advantage of the empty streets to speed along, but it only took them ten minutes or so before he pulled up outside a club in a street near the river with the discreet sign 'Purdey's' over the door. They got out and waited for Gerald to join them.

Inside it wasn't a terribly large place, just a biggish room with galleries on two sides, set out with tables and chairs facing a small stage which at the moment had the curtains drawn. Nearly all the tables were full, the customers chatting over their drinks or listening to a four-piece band who played background music in a corner. A smiling waiter led them down the stairs into the main room and showed them to a table. Minta looked round her interestedly; she hadn't known the place existed before. There seemed to be an expectant air in the place; everyone kept looking towards the stage, and she wondered just what kind of a show Dane had brought them to see.

A waiter came to take their order and Dane asked for champagne.

'Just what is this place?' Gerald demanded morosely. 'A strip club?' Most of the people were in evening dress and he felt completely out of place in his riding breeches.

'Sorry to disappoint you,' Dane answered lightly. 'You'll see in a minute.'

The waiter brought their drinks, and after a few minutes Minta noticed that all the waiters had gone up to the gallery level and were gathered on a small balcony near the doorway. The band finished its number and the musicians disappeared into some back room. Immediately an expectant hush filled the room and everyone turned their chairs so that they could get their best view of the stage. The lights dimmed until it was almost dark except for a strong spotlight directed at the centre of the stage. The heavy curtains parted, but to Minta's surprise there was no stage setting, just another black curtain a few feet behind the other. Then a white-gloved hand parted the curtain. A collective sigh of pleasure ran through the audience.

It was a mime show given by four mummers wearing jet black costumes that blended into the black curtain, only their faces, with chalk white make-up, and their white-gloved hands showing. But what they did was brilliant. Minta sat entranced as she watched the hands become birds, then snapping dogs or purring cats, and the white faces told silent stories, so sad that she wanted to cry, and sometimes so funny that the whole audience burst into spontaneous laughter and she laughed so much that tears came to her eyes anyway.

She groped for her bag to find a handkerchief, but found one put into her hand. 'Enjoying it?' Dane asked softly.

'It's marvellous.' She dabbed at her eyes and gave the handkerchief back, found him looking at her with a strange, almost contemplative look in his eyes, which quickly changed to a smile. Then she turned to watch the stage again, but it was a few minutes before she was wholly absorbed.

The show lasted for over an hour, which went by like minutes, and ended to thunderous applause and repeated calls for more, but after they had taken their eighth bow the curtain came down on the mummers and stayed firmly closed.

'That was absolutely brilliant!' Minta gave a sigh of pleasure and turned to Dane, her eyes warm. 'Thank you so much for bringing us here. How on earth did you find it when you live so far away? I've never heard of the place before.'

'I come over to London quite a lot on business. Someone brought me here on a previous visit.'

'It was great. And you were right; I did enjoy it—much more.' Dane smiled and lifted his glass to clink it against hers.

'Much more than what?' Gerald interrupted brusquely.

'What? Oh, just something we were talking about earlier.'

'I see.' Gerald looked at them both sourly, quite rightly thinking that he was gradually being excluded.

Dane turned to him and courteously asked him about himself; what he did, that kind of thing.

'I help my father to run his estates,' Gerald answered shortly. 'That and his other business interests.' Adding, in the hope of putting Dane down, 'Running a large estate is quite a responsibility, you know.'

'Yes,' Dane agreed casually. 'So I found when I inherited mine.'

There was a loud silence which Minta broke by asking, 'Was that in the Canary Islands?'

'Yes, mostly in Gran Canaria. My grandmother, you see, came from the Canary Islands and brought a lot of land there into the family, but my grandfather's side of the family have always lived in Warwickshire.'

Minta was about to ask him why he didn't live in Warwickshire now, but then remembered that he had mentioned an older brother; presumably he had inherited the main property in England and Dane had been left with that in the Canary Islands.

'Does—does your wife mind living there?' Minta asked hesitantly.

He didn't smile or look amused, but answered steadily, 'I'm not married.'

Gerald stood up. 'Everyone's leaving and it's time I took Minta home.'

Looking round, Minta saw that the audience had gradually broken up, drifting away in twos and fours. She glanced at her watch, saw that it was gone two and gave an exclamation of surprise. 'Good heavens, I'd no idea it was so late. The time has just flown by.'

'Do you really want to go home?' Dane asked her. 'Or would you like to go on to Tramps for supper?'

Again there was that challenge in his grey eyes and this time she didn't even bother to think about it. 'Oh, yes, please. I'd love that.'

'Good.' He put a hand under her elbow and helped her to her feet. 'Coming, Gerald?'

'Minta ought to go home,' Gerald protested. 'Her father doesn't like her to be out too late.'

'Oh, Gerald, don't be so stuffy! You know I often stay out later than this.'

His mouth set into a mutinous line and as soon as they got outside he took hold of her arm and pulled her unwillingly towards his car. 'We'll go in mine,' he said forcefully.

'All right, you don't have to hurt me,' Minta complained, trying to drag her arm away.

They set off following Dane's car, but Gerald let it get ahead and then turned off in a different direction.

'Hey! This isn't the way. Where are you going?'

'I'm taking you home,' Gerald muttered. 'I've had quite enough tonight.'

'But I want to go to Tramps.'

'Too bad,' he replied rudely.

'Will you please turn this car round and take me to Tramps?'

'No, I darn well won't.'

'All right. Then as soon as we get back to my place I'll get in my car and drive there myself!'

'Just because you want to join Fenton, I suppose?'

'And why not—he's my father's guest?'

'Well, he darn well isn't mine. Who the hell does he think he is, pushing his way into our date like that? And just who is it you want to be with—him or me?' Gerald demanded, really angry now.

Minta hadn't thought about that before and she didn't think about it now as she answered hotly, 'Him, if you must know. You're getting to be a real bore, Gerald. And pompous, too. You should have heard yourself when you said that "running an estate is quite a responsibility, you know",' she said, mimicking his voice and looking down her nose.

Gerald's face suffused with colour. He stamped on the brakes, then turned the car round and headed back fast in the direction in which they'd come. 'All right,' he said furiously. 'If that's the way you feel you can go ahead and throw yourself at some stranger who's going to laugh himself silly when he goes back to his precious Canary Islands. And don't try and make it up with me when he leaves you high and dry!'

They came in sight of Tramps and he drew up with a jerk in front of it. Dane was standing waiting on the pavement outside, quietly smoking a cigarette which he threw away as he opened the door for Minta. 'Get held up in the traffic?' he asked Gerald sardonically. But Gerald merely reached over to slam the door shut and roared away.

Dane watched him go with cool amusement. 'I wondered how long it would take before he got the message.'

'You mean you wanted him to go?'

He glanced down at her, his eyes resting on her face. 'Of course.'

'We had a terrible row in the car,' Minta admitted.

He put a hand on her arm and drew her towards him. 'The row was inevitable. Better to have it in his car than in the middle of the dance floor.'

'Why there?'

'Because that was the only place I was going to let him have a chance of being alone with you.'

Minta stared at him, not really understanding. She gave a little, embarrassed laugh. 'Well, now I'm afraid you'll have to put up with me by yourself.'

'I know. It's what I intended all along.' Putting up a hand, he gently traced the outline of her cheek and along her jawline, tipping up her chin so that she had to look directly at him. 'And you're going to have to get used to having just me around.'

'Oh?' Minta felt suddenly breathless. 'Why?'

'Don't you know?' He was leaning nearer, his eyes fixed on her face.

She tried to shake her head, but he was still holding her 'N-no,' she stammered, her heart hammering in her chest.

Slowly he bent and gently kissed her, his lips firm again her mouth. 'Because,' he said deliberately, 'we're going to get married.'

CHAPTER TWO

MINTA'S mouth came open and stayed that way as she stared at him, until Dane, with an amused smile, lifted her chin and closed it for her.

'You're—you're crazy,' she stammered.

'That's right, I am,' he agreed. 'About you.'

'But you don't know me!' she exclaimed.

'Then we'll have the rest of our lives to get to know each other,' he told her flippantly, but then his eyes grew serious. 'How long does it really take to find out you love someone, Minta? Okay, perhaps for some it takes months or even years, but for others it need only be minutes or hours.' He gave a short laugh. 'Maybe I didn't believe those stories about love at first sight before, but I certainly do now. One look at you and I was knocked for six. I still feel punch-drunk.'

'You—you *really* fell in love with me?' Minta still couldn't believe it.

He put his hands on her shoulders. 'I *really* fell in love with you.'

Behind them the double doors to the night club opened and a noisy group of people came out.

'Look, do you still want to go in there and have supper?' asked Dane, and when Minta shook her head rather dazedly, he put an arm round her waist. 'Let's walk, then.'

It was a chill November night with a touch of frost on the ground, but Minta didn't feel the cold. They walked slowly along, close together, Dane keeping his arm around her. He was quite a bit taller and she had to look up at him all the time.

'I know this has taken you by surprise,' he told her. 'Maybe I shouldn't have said anything yet; should have waited and given you time to get to know how you felt about me. I don't want to rush you into anything, but . . .' He stopped abruptly, then swung her round to face him. 'Yes, I do,' he said forcefully, his hands gripping her arms. 'I very much want to rush you into marrying me. I love you, Minta. And I told you because I'm hoping against hope that you feel the same. If the miracle happened to me then surely it did to you too. The gods wouldn't be cruel enough to only make it happen to one of us. Would they, my darling? Would they?' he demanded urgently.

She gazed up at him, her heart thumping painfully, her hands beginning to shake. 'Oh, Dane, I . . .' She found it difficult to speak.

He gave a kind of groan. 'You don't have to say it. I should have known it was too much to hope.'

He went to turn away from her dejectedly, but Minta caught his sleeve. 'Wait. Look at me, please.' His eyes came up, devouring her face. Hesitantly she said, 'I've never been in love before—I don't know what it's like. But I feel excited and sort of bubbly inside. And I—and I feel as if I want to touch you—and be touched by you.' She paused, her cheeks flushed. 'And I feel as if I want you to take care of me; that I'd be safe with you. Is—is that love?'

Dane put his hands gently on either side of her face. 'When I think of the future,' he said softly, 'I can't imagine it without you. Do you feel like that?'

'Yes,' Minta whispered on a note of wonder. 'Yes, I do.'

'Then the gods have been kind, my darling, because the miracle has happened to you, too.'

'There's something else I feel,' she said slowly. 'I would very much like you to kiss me again.'

He smiled and slowly lowered his hands to draw her close to him, then bent his head to seek her lips. There was no hurry in the way he kissed her, his mouth lingered, gently exploring, his lips caressing the soft fullness of hers, as if getting to know her, like someone slowly unwrapping a present in the joy of prolonging the anticipation. Minta sighed, her mouth moving against his, and put her arms around his neck. Immediately his arms tightened and his kiss became deeper, more demanding. She didn't attempt to resist, she let herself be carried along on the rising tide of his passion.

'Oh, my dearest, dearest girl!' He kissed her eyes, her throat, his breath scorching her skin. 'If you only knew how long I've waited for someone like you! I was beginning to think it would never happen to me.'

Minta clung to him, her body on fire, murmuring his name over and over again, almost overcome by emotion. And there wasn't a doubt in her mind. After the first shock of realisation she had accepted her own feelings and Dane's too. Accepted it as the simple miracle he said it was. But it was intoxicating, overwhelming; she had never known such exhilarating excitement.

And he must have felt it too, because he threw back his head and laughed aloud, then lifted her in his strong arms and swung her round, his handsome face alight with happiness. 'To think I came to London for just a routine business trip and I found the one girl in the whole world that I want to spend the rest of my life with!' He set her down on her feet and put a hand on her shoulder, his mood suddenly changing as he gazed into her face. 'Promise me that you'll never change your mind. If I lost you now . . . God, I couldn't bear it!'

'I won't,' she assured him. 'I know this is right. I want to be with you always.'

'Oh, my dearest love!' He kissed her again and it was some time before either of them became aware of their surroundings, and the kisses were much too hot for them to feel the cold. But eventually Dane released her sufficiently for them to walk slowly along again, his arm round her waist. Minta felt as if she was walking on air.

Their wandering steps carried them to Trafalgar Square where the huge bronze lions stood guard over the column of England's dead hero. Frost glittered on their smooth backs, reflected into a million glistening diamonds by the lamplight. The pigeons who lived there during the day had sought shelter on the surrounding buildings and there were no night birds to break the silence. Tacitly they paused at the entrance to the square and Dane unbuttoned his overcoat and, holding her close against his side, put it round her to help keep her warm.

Minta snuggled against him. 'I'll always remember tonight,' she murmured, looking out across the square.

Dane stooped to kiss her cold nose. 'Will you mind going to the Canary Islands to live with me?'

She didn't hesitate. 'No. I'll go anywhere with you. Whither thou goest, I will go,' she quoted softly.

A triumphant light came into Dane's eyes. 'You won't mind leaving England?'

'No. But we'll come back here often, won't we?' For the first time she thought of her father and there was a trace of anxiety in her voice.

'Yes, of course. Whenever you want. Darling, I can't wait to take you there, to show you my home,' he exclaimed impetuously. 'I know you'll love it. We must get married soon so that I can take you back with me.'

Minta gave a gasping laugh. 'Hey, give me time to get used to the idea! I don't know what my father will say to all this.'

'Does it matter? You're of age, aren't you?' There was an anxious note in his voice.

'Yes, of course; I'm twenty-one. But Daddy's bound to think it sudden. He's sure to want me to wait and get to know you better.'

'But what is there to wait for?' Dane protested. 'Time will only make us love each other more. And I want you, Minta.' His arms tightened round her urgently. 'I want you for my wife. I've waited so long already; don't make me go on waiting just to pay lip-service to conventionality. Ours isn't that kind of love, my darling. Ours is a once-in-a-lifetime.'

'Oh, I know—I know. I don't want to wait either. Oh, Dane!' Minta clung to him as he kissed her hungrily, his lips fierce. He held her very close against him, and she could feel the hardness of his body. It sent such a flame of desire shooting through her that she gave a gasping cry and moved her hips against his. He withstood it for a few moments, then abruptly released her and stepped away. 'God!' he muttered unsteadily. 'Do you know what you're doing to me?'

'You're having quite an effect on me too,' Minta pointed out.

Dane laughed and took her hand in his. 'If only this were America and we could just go to the nearest chapel and be married without any delay or fuss. Then we could . . .'

He stopped and didn't go on, but Minta knew exactly what he was going to say: 'Then we could go to bed together and make love tonight.' She flushed and her hand tightened on his. 'I know. I—I feel that way, too.'

This time he didn't say anything, just kissed her on her forehead and then on the mouth, before again wrapping her in his coat and starting to walk through the square. They didn't talk a great deal, they both felt that there was plenty of time for that, all they wanted to do was hold each other close, as if by holding each other they could also hold this moment in time and make it go on forever.

The darkness of night was giving way to the first weak light of dawn when they at last reached Minta's home. Dane looked up at the dark windows of the house. 'Which is your room?'

She pointed it out to him. 'There—on the first floor to the left.'

'Tell me about the room so that I can think of you there.'

Minta started to describe it, but after a few sentences her voice trailed away. He was looking at her so intently, with such need in his eyes. 'Oh, Dane, I don't want to leave you.'

He kissed her then as if he would never let her go, only reluctantly raising his head. 'You'll come out with me tomorrow?'

'Yes, of course,' she agreed breathlessly, her heart still hammering from his embrace. 'But I don't even know where you're staying?'

'At the Cumberland. Don't say anything to your father yet—I want to be with you when you do. I'll call you tomorrow.'

'All right. I ought to go in,' she told him reluctantly.

'In a minute.' But the minute turned out to be ten as he kissed her again and again, at last groaning as he forcibly put her from him. 'You'd better go in or I'll never let you go.'

Her head in a whirl, Minta climbed the steps and somehow found her key in her handbag. She opened the door and stood there for a moment, looking down at his dark handsomeness, still unable to believe that it was true. Impulsively she ran down the steps and threw her arms round his neck. 'Oh, Dane, I love you so much!' Then she quickly kissed him with unleashed passion before running inside.

The house was very quiet. Minta crept through it, afraid of waking her father—and Maggie, if she'd stayed the night. Once in her room, she turned on the light, and immediately crossed to the window. Dane was still outside. She blew him a kiss and watched him wave and walk away, hunched in his overcoat, before she drew the curtains. She undressed quickly, her heart still singing, her mind a whirl of happiness, almost glad to be alone because she rather thought her poor heart was about to burst and couldn't take any more. But although she got into bed fully determined to go over the night again, sleep claimed her almost at once and she slept on until late in the morning.

She awoke reluctantly, like someone who has had a wonderful dream and desperately wants to go back to it, shutting her eyes and groping for the memory. But then she realised that her dream was real and immediately sat up, grabbing at her bedside clock. 'Oh, no!' She shot out of bed when she saw it was gone eleven and rushed into the bathroom. Quickly she washed and dressed and ran downstairs. Only the housekeeper, Mrs Doyle, was around.

'Have there been any phone calls for me?' Minta demanded as she burst into the kitchen.

'Good morning.' Mrs Doyle looked at her reprovingly as she cleaned the silver they had used at the dinner party last night.

'Sorry, Doyley, I didn't mean to be rude—but have there been any calls for me?' she asked anxiously.

'A couple. I told them you were still in bed and they both said they'd ring back.'

'But who were they from? Was it the same man?'

'What makes you think it was a man?'

'Oh, Doyley, don't tease, please! This is important.'

Surprised by the urgency in her tone, the housekeeper answered, 'I'm not sure; neither of them gave their name, but it didn't sound like the same man.' She got to her feet. 'Do you want something to eat? It's a bit late for breakfast.'

'Just coffee will do, thanks.' Minta sat on the opposite side of the table, looking at the wall phone and willing it to ring.

Doyley set a mug of coffee and a slice of chocolate cake in front of her, before sitting down again. 'Here you are. You look happy this morning.'

'I am.' Minta gave her a radiant smile. 'Wonderfully happy.'

'Gerald didn't propose, did he?' The older woman paused in her work.

'Who—Gerald? Good heavens, no! I wouldn't marry Gerald in a million years!' Minta exclaimed, appalled at the thought.

'I thought you were keen on him?'

'Oh, no. He's a bore.'

'So you've met someone else, have you? Who is it this time?'

Minta found that she didn't want to share Dane with anyone, not yet. Trying to sound offhand, she said, 'Oh, no one in particular. I'm just glad to be free of Gerald, that's all.'

'I see,' Doyley said drily. 'And that's why you can't wait for the phone to ring, is it? So that you can talk to no one in particular?'

Minta grinned sheepishly and was about to answer when the phone really did ring, making her jump. She put down her coffee mug so hastily that she spilt some on the pine table. 'I'll take it in Daddy's study,' she called out, already halfway to the door. But when she picked up the phone, she was overwhelmingly disappointed to hear Gerald's voice answer her eager greeting. 'Oh, it's you.' She made no effort to hide her feelings, but Gerald was too thick-skinned to notice.

'Of course it is. Didn't your housekeeper tell you that I phoned earlier?'

'You didn't leave your name. How was she supposed to know who you were?'

'Look, about last night. I'm sorry I went off and left you alone with Fenton. You must have been bored out of your mind.'

'No,' Minta replied, hardly able to keep the laughter out of her voice, 'I wasn't bored.'

'Oh.' He sounded disconcerted. 'Well, I suppose I shouldn't have left you, but I didn't like him tagging along. After all, it was hardly Fenton's scene; he was much too old for De Sade',' implying by his tone that Dane was also much too old for her. 'And that mime show he took us to!' Gerald sounded disgusted. 'That was for octogenarians up.'

'I liked it,' she informed him. 'Look, Gerald, is this

for anything specific, because I'm expecting an important call?'

Huffily he said, 'I told you: to apologise, and to tell you I've got tickets for the rock concert tonight. I'll pick you up at seven.'

'Sorry,' Minta replied shortly. 'I'm busy tonight.'

'Well, I suppose I could change them for tomorrow instead.'

'I'm busy tomorrow, too. In fact, Gerald, I'm going to be busy for the rest of my life, so please don't waste your time calling me again. 'Bye.' She put the phone down on his rising note of protest.

She laughed happily and did a twirling dance in the small confines of the room. The phone rang again almost immediately and for a moment she didn't answer it, thinking that it must be Gerald refusing to take no for an answer, but then she picked it up just on the offchance, and was instantly rewarded.

'Hallo, sleepyhead. How's my wonderful girl this morning?' Dane's deep voice was as warm as a caress.

'I feel as if I'm still asleep, as if last night was only a dream.'

'So do I. Why don't we meet so that we can pinch each other and make sure we're awake?'

'Of course. When and where?'

'I have an appointment shortly, but I should be finished in time for lunch. Why don't we meet at one o'clock at the Cumberland and we'll have lunch there?'

'That sounds fine.' Minta gave a happy sigh. 'Oh, Dane, I can't wait to see you again!'

'Nor I, darling. You haven't had second thoughts since last night?'

'Oh, no! And you haven't, have you?' she asked anxiously, for a brief and terrible second envisaging what life would be like without him.

'Are you crazy? My every waking thought has been of you. The people I've had to meet today must think I'm an idiot, the way I keep forgetting why I'm supposed to be there. Darn, they're asking for me now. Sorry, Minta, I'll have to go. See you at one, darling.'

Minta flew upstairs to change, even though she had loads of time. She sang happily as she bathed and tried on a dozen different outfits before she made up her mind what to wear. At twelve-thirty she took a taxi to the Cumberland, too impatient to sit at home and wait, hoping that Dane, too, might be early so that they could have an extra few minutes together. But he was a little late, and Minta was anxiously scanning every new arrival when he finally pushed through the swing doors. Then he strode quickly across to her and she jumped to her feet and waved.

'Darling!' He took her in his arms and kissed her, oblivious of everyone around them. 'You don't know how much I've longed for this moment, to look at you again, touch you, convince myself that you're real.'

Minta laughed shakily. 'I feel exactly the same way. Don't let me go, will you?'

'I promise.' He tucked her arm through his. 'Let's go in the bar and have a drink while we decide what to eat.' They sat down and were given menus to study, but neither of them was really interested. Dane kept a tight hold on her hand and said, 'I'm sorry I was late. I had a hell of a job getting away from my meeting, and then I got held up in the traffic. I was cursing every moment it kept me away from you.'

'You haven't told me yet why you're in England,' Minta reminded him.

He shrugged off the question. 'Just family business. But the point is, my love, that I can only stay here ten days at the most, then I simply must go back to the Canaries.'

'Only ten days?' She looked at him in dismay.

'Yes. Of course I have various business meetings fixed up that I have to go to, but I'll spend as much time with you as I can.' The waiter came up to take their order and they realised they hadn't even looked at the menu. Dane glanced at it abstractedly. 'Oh—we'll have the salmon, followed by tournedos and whatever vegetables are in season. Is that okay with you, darling?'

'Yes, anything.' Minta was overcome by the way he called her darling so naturally, as if they'd known each other for years; and anyway she was sure she wouldn't be able to eat anything.

The huge dining-room of the Cumberland Hotel was already crowded and neither of them minded being shown to a small table tucked into an alcove where they could hold hands across the table and forget everyone else around them.

'Ten days is an awfully short time,' Minta said unhappily.

'But it could be enough,' Dane pointed out, looking at her steadily, 'if you'll trust me.'

'Enough—for what?' But she already knew what he was going to say and her heart began to race crazily.

'For us to get married.' He brought both his hands to cover hers. 'Darling, I know it's rushing you, but what is there to wait for? I'm sure in my own mind, and if you are too . . .'

'I *am*,' she assured him. 'But it's Daddy. He's bound to object at our only knowing each other such a short time. Couldn't we wait perhaps a couple of months? You could come back to England as often as you can.'

'Do you *want* to wait a couple of months?' Dane asked softly, his eyes frankly caressing.

'Minta gulped. 'No. Oh, no!'

'And it might not be possible,' he sighed. 'If my business in London is successful, then yes, I'll be able to come back here after a few weeks. But if it's not then I'll have to go to Spain and France, and possibly America, before I'll be free to come to England again.'

Minta's face paled. 'How long would all that take?'

He shrugged rather helplessly. 'It could be months.'

Their food came, but neither of them had an appetite. Minta felt close to tears; to have found such wonderful happiness and then to have to so soon face being separated for an indefinite length of time was more than she could bear. 'When will you know?' she asked, clutching at straws.

'Not for nearly a week.' His grey eyes searched her face and his hand gripped hers. 'In a week we could be married.'

Minta's throat went dry as she stared back at him. She wished they were married now. She wished they could go up to his room and make love. Never had she known such intense physical desire. It made her hand tremble and her heart race. And she knew then that she would marry Dane next week, whatever the outcome of his business deals, because there was no way she was going to be parted from him, even for a few weeks while he went back to the Canaries. Dane started to speak again, but the waiter came to fill up their wine glasses and he had to let go her hand, which was probably just as well.

When the waiter had gone, Minta said shakily, 'All—all right. We'll get married before you go back home.'

'Minta!' Dane picked up her hand and carried it to his lips, then groaned. 'God, if only we were alone so that I could show you how I feel!'

'Show me later,' she smiled shakily.

His eyes became ardent. 'Oh, I will, don't worry.'

'I'll—I'll tell Daddy tonight.'

'No, not yet. Give it a few more days so that I can see how things work out. But in the meantime you'd better give me your birth certificate so that I can get a special licence. And when the time comes to tell your father, either I'll see him alone or we'll tell him together. Okay?'

'Okay.' She nodded in some relief; much as she loved her father, her imagination cringed at the thought of his anger when he heard she wanted to marry a man she hardly knew.

Dane had another meeting fixed for that afternoon. 'I have to see your father again, as a matter of fact,' he told her. So after they had eaten they had only a short time together before he called a taxi. They went first to her house where Minta ran inside to the study, found her birth certificate in the drawer where all the family documents were kept, and ran out again to give it to Dane. The idea had been that he would drop her off, but she couldn't bear to be apart from him, so she drove back with him into the City. 'I'll call for you tonight,' he told her. 'About seven.' He went to give her a light kiss on the cheek, but Minta turned her face to his.

'Kiss me properly,' she pleaded huskily, her hands gripping his jacket. 'Please!'

Dane gave a quick glance in the taxi-driver's direction, but the man wasn't looking at them. Putting his arms around her, he drew her towards him, his mouth finding hers caressingly. 'Don't you realise what an effect kissing you properly has on me?' he murmured.

'Of course I do. And I'm glad.' Her hands slid inside his jacket, began to undo his shirt.

'Minx!' Suddenly his kiss hardened, turned to passion, and he bore her back against the seat, not letting up until she was breathless. Then he raised his head and smiled at her bemused face. 'Was that what you call kissing you properly?'

'Oh, *yes*!'

He grinned again. 'It wasn't, you know. Given the right time and place I can do a lot better than that.' Then he looked at his watch. 'Oh, hell! I *must* go, or I'll be late to see your father. 'Bye, darling.' One more kiss and then he dragged himself away, thrusting some money into the driver's hand and hurrying into the bank.

Minta leant back in her seat and put up a trembling hand to touch her lips, still tender from the passion of his kiss. If he could do better than that . . . Wow! She wondered what he'd meant by the right time and place—and could make a pretty accurate guess. She imagined herself going to bed with him—what it would be like.

'Where to, miss?' The taxi-driver's impatient voice broke through her reverie, bringing a hot flush to her cheeks.

'What? Oh! Er . . . Knightsbridge, please.'

Ten minutes later the taxi dropped her off in the fashionable shopping centre and she spent the rest of the afternoon buying the sexiest nightdresses and underwear she could find.

'For your trousseau, madam?' one assistant asked her as she wrapped the delicate, lace-encrusted undies.

'Why, yes. Yes, they are.' And only as she said it did Minta actually realise it was true. She was going to be married. She would be Dane's wife. Mrs Fenton. Araminta Fenton. She said the names in her mind, trying them out and finding them entirely to her liking. Mrs Dane Fenton. Yes, that was how it sounded best of all.

That evening they went out for a meal to an exclusive French restaurant. 'How did your meeting with my father go?' Minta asked Dane eagerly.

He gave a slight shrug. 'Not quite as well as I'd hoped. He and his co-directors are hard men to do business with. But nothing's settled yet. We may still be able to come to terms.'

'I wish I could help,' Minta said wistfully. 'Perhaps if I told him I was going out with you?'

He lifted a quizzical eyebrow. 'Do you really think that that would influence your father's business attitude?'

Regretfully, she shook her head. 'No, not at all.'

Lifting her hand to his lips, Dane kissed each finger one by one, then turned her hand so that he could kiss her palm. 'Do you know that you're very, very sweet?'

'Sweet enough to—to eat?' she asked breathlessly; having her palm kissed like that was a real turn-on.

His eyes came up to meet hers, hold them. 'I think you already know the answer to that one,' he said softly.

Her hand tightened convulsively on his. 'Oh, Dane, I love you so much!'

'Then you won't object to wearing this.' Gently he freed his hand and took a small box from his pocket. Inside it was an exquisite opal ring, surrounded by diamonds. Picking up her left hand, he slowly slid the ring on to her third finger.

Minta looked at the jewel sparkling with muted fire on her hand and silly tears came to her eyes, and such a lump in her throat that she couldn't speak.

'I hope you like it,' Dane prompted, apprehensive at her silence.

'I love it! It's beautiful.' She flung her arms round his neck and hugged him, much to the amusement of people sitting at the nearby tables. 'I just feel so—so choked up inside.'

'Darling!' He put up a hand to brush away her tears, and when she had got over it a little, said, 'Does it fit? If not I can . . .'

'It fits fine,' Minta said hastily, although in fact it was a little large, but there was no way she was going to take it off.

'Good. And I've put matters in hand to get a special licence. We should be able to marry in five days' time.'

'That's next Tuesday.'

'Yes.' Dane grinned. 'Or we can wait a couple more days if you want a really long engagement.'

Minta laughed with him, then said, 'Why is it, do you think, that we're so lucky? That we two should be singled out to meet and fall in love so quickly? Why doesn't it happen to everyone this way?'

'I don't know.' He tilted her chin to look into her eyes, his own very tender. 'Maybe we're blessed by the gods. But I know that I'm the luckiest man alive.'

They spent the rest of the evening at a cinema, holding hands, hardly aware of the film, wishing they could be alone. When they came out it was very cold after the warm fug of the cinema, and Minta shivered.

'I'll be glad to get you home to the Canaries where it's warm,' Dane remarked, shrugging himself into his overcoat.

'Why, is it summer there? I've never been to the Canaries.'

'No, but we have a very temperate climate all the year round. They call them the islands of eternal spring. You can get a suntan there at any time. Where would you like to go now?' he added. 'It's too cold to just walk.'

Impetuously Minta exclaimed, 'I know! Daddy's taking Maggie out tonight and he'll probably stay at her flat. Why don't we go back to my place? It will be warm there and we can—have a drink, or something.' She didn't add that she wanted desperately to be alone with him, but it was written large in her eyes.

The house was in darkness when they arrived. They took off their coats in the hall and Minta led the way to the sitting-room, turned on a couple of lamps and poked the fire until it gave a bright glow. There was no need to be careful not to wake Doyley; the housekeeper lived out and only came in at eight every morning.

Dane sat down on the settee in front of the fire and, catching her wrist, pulled her down on to his lap. 'Come here, woman.'

Minta went, more than willingly. Kicking off her shoes, she snuggled up to him, her hands going inside his jacket. 'Do you have a hairy chest?' she demanded.

He looked dismayed. 'Is that a condition of marriage?'

She pretended to consider, then, 'No, I guess I'll take you as you are.'

'Thank God for that; there's no way I could have grown a mat of hair by Tuesday.'

'You haven't got any?'

'Not one.' He shook his head.

'Show me,' Minta demanded flirtatiously.

'Okay—but only if you'll show me yours.'

Minta gurgled with laughter. She put her arms round his neck and grew suddenly serious again. 'You have the strangest effect on me, you know that? One minute I'm so happy I could burst and the next I want to cry.'

'There's a very simple diagnosis for that; you're obviously in love. And there's an even simpler remedy.'

'There is?'

'Yes. It's this.' Putting a hand behind her head, Dane drew her towards him and kissed her hungrily, then he leant her back against the arm of the settee, his lips growing ever more forceful.

Minta responded ardently, her mouth moving against his, touching, caressing—incredibly tantalising, incredibly sexy. His hands began to explore her body, lifting her sweater and finding the soft silkiness of her skin. She sighed as his mouth left hers and moved on to explore her throat, her body on fire with desire, moving sensuously under his hands. Unhooking her bra, Dane pushed it aside and raised his head to look at her, his eyes dark. Delicately he began to stroke and caress her with his fingertips, the feather-light touch driving her wild. 'Dane! Oh God, Dane!' Her body arched, thrusting up towards him, her nipples hardening. 'Kiss me there. Oh, please kiss me there.'

He didn't obey her immediately but played with her for a little longer until she thought she'd go crazy, then

he slowly lowered his head and used his tongue instead
of his fingers. Minta gasped, her fingers digging into his
shoulders, for the moment overwhelmed by the
wonderful sensations he was arousing in her, but the
need for fulfilment growing ever stronger. But then
Dane lifted his head.

'Don't stop. Oh, please don't stop,' Minta begged.

'Listen.' He put a warning hand gently over her
mouth.

Somehow she dragged herself back to reality and
became aware of someone in the hall. Then a voice
called out, 'Minta, are you home?'

'It's Daddy!' Quickly she sat up and fumbled her way
into her bra, pulled down her sweater. Dane caught her
hand and slipped the engagement ring from her finger,
then straightened his tie and pushed a hand through his
dishevelled hair.

'In—in here,' Minta called out, hastily going over to
the drinks tray and starting to pour out a couple of
gins. Her father came into the room and Dane got to
his feet, apparently quite unconcerned. 'Hallo again,' he
said easily.

Richard Tennant looked more than a little surprised
to see him. 'Why, Fenton! Has something happened?
Did you want to see me again?' He glanced at his
watch, completely puzzled.

Dane smiled. 'No, nothing like that. I took Minta out
to dinner to say thank you for the excellent meal she
gave me last night, and she kindly invited me back for a
nightcap.'

'I see.' His eyes travelled from Dane to Minta, rested
for a few contemplative seconds on her flushed face. 'I
might as well join you, then. Whisky and soda, please,
darling.'

Minta obediently poured out the drink, glad to turn her back on him. She carried them over and Dane gave her a small grin of encouragement as she handed him his glass.

'Have you been somewhere interesting?' Her father sat in his favourite armchair, crossing his legs and making himself comfortable. Minta's heart sank; she knew those signs, it meant that he was determined to outsit whoever she had invited back. It had happened several times before when he didn't know or approve of some boy-friend.

Dane answered him casually enough and the two men chatted for about twenty minutes, with Minta only joining in occasionally, but Dane must have realised that her father intended to stay because, as soon as he had finished his drink, he stood up. 'If you'll excuse me, I must be getting back to my hotel.' He smiled at Minta and her heart gave a crazy lurch. 'Thank you for taking pity on me.'

'Nonsense. Thank you for a very pleasant evening.' She tried to keep her voice light.

He shook hands with her father and wished him goodnight.

Minta said, 'I'll see you out,' holding the door open and shutting it firmly behind them. 'I'm sorry,' she whispered as he put on his coat. 'I really thought he wouldn't be back tonight.'

'Not to worry. Here, you'd better hide this.' He gave her the ring and she slipped it into the pocket of her full skirt. 'I'll call you tomorrow. Goodnight, darling.'

They snatched a brief, passionate kiss and then he put up his collar against the cold and hurried to his car.

Reluctantly Minta put her head round the sitting-room door. 'Goodnight, Daddy. See you tomorrow.'

'Just a minute; I'd like to have a word with you.'

'Oh, not now,' she pouted. 'I'm tired. You can tell me tomorrow.'

'It won't take long,' Richard Tennant insisted. 'Come and sit down by the fire.'

Slowly Minta obeyed him, but she didn't sit at his feet as she did on other nights, instead sitting where Dane had sat, feeling the warmth of his body on the cushions. Her father opened his mouth to speak, but she forestalled him by saying, 'I thought you were going out with Maggie tonight?'

'I did, but she developed a headache, so I took her home.'

'And she didn't want you to stay and comfort her?' Minta asked rather waspishly, still resentful of his having walked in on them.

'Not tonight, no.' His voice hardened. 'Fenton didn't mention that he was seeing you tonight when we met this afternoon.'

'Didn't he?' Minta tried hard to sound offhand. 'I expect he's like you and doesn't mix business with pleasure.'

'Are you going to see him again?'

'That's rather up to him, isn't it?'

'Hardly—in this day and age,' he remarked drily. He studied her averted face for a moment, then said, 'I'd rather you didn't go out with him again, Minta.'

'Oh? Why?'

'He's trying to negotiate a deal with the bank. It might make things awkward if you get friendly with him.'

'I don't see why,' Minta retorted hotly. 'Gerald's father is a bank customer and you didn't object to me going out with him. In fact you encouraged me to.'

'The circumstances are different, but I can't go into detail, you know that. Sorry, darling, but I'm going to have to insist that you don't see Fenton again.'

'That's ridiculous!' Minta jumped angrily to her feet. 'You were the one who brought him here and introduced him to me.'

'I know, but I hadn't talked to him then, found out what he wanted. He was just a potential customer.'

'Well, that's just too bad. Because I intend to see him just as often as I like. And I couldn't care less whether he's a customer of your precious bank or not!'

Her father, too, was annoyed now, but he had had more practice at holding it in check. Getting to his feet, he came over and put a placating hand on her arm. 'Now, let's try and talk this over calmly. There's really no need to get so worked up about it.'

Minta jerked her arm away. 'I'm going to see him again! You needn't try and persuade me—make me see reason, as you call it. Nothing you say will make any difference.'

He stared at her, taken aback by her vehemence. 'You must like him a lot,' he observed slowly.

'Yes, I do. I like him so much that I . . .' For a moment she was on the point of telling him everything; not only was she angry, but also she had always confided in her father and subconsciously wanted his approval now, but her promise to Dane held her back. 'That I shall go out with him whenever he asks me,' she finished, her chin coming up defiantly.

Richard Tennant was the senior director of a highly successful merchant bank and was used to having his orders obeyed without question, especially by his juniors. Now he made the fatal mistake of expecting his daughter to do the same. His voice rising, he said harshly, 'You will do as you're told. You are not to get involved with Dane Fenton. Do you understand?'

Minta stared at him, unused to having him use that tone with her now that she was grown up. Colour flamed in her cheeks as she glared back at him. 'Well, that's just too bad,' she retorted angrily. 'Because you're too late—I already am involved with him.'

'And just what is that supposed to mean?' he demanded explosively.

'It means just whatever you want to think it does!' Furiously Minta turned on her heel and slammed out of the room. Ignoring his barked command to come back, she ran upstairs to her bedroom, locking the door firmly behind her.

CHAPTER THREE

FOR several minutes Minta stood by the door, listening, afraid that her father would follow her and demand to have it out, but he stayed downstairs and she eventually went to sit on her bed, still trembling with anger. Taking the ring from her pocket, she sat looking at it for a long time, then put it back on her finger, turning her hand so that the light caught the jewels and enhanced their brilliance. Kicking off her shoes, she lay back on the bed, still fully dressed, her mind far too full to even think of sleep. Uppermost, of course, was the row with her father. It was the last thing she had wanted, but he had more or less forced it on her when he had taken that dictatorial attitude. Even if she hadn't been in love with Dane she would have resented such heavy-handed interference. And it wasn't like him; usually they had a good relationship and could talk things over until they reached an agreement, but tonight he had hardly even attempted to discuss the situation, had just issued a peremptory order. Perhaps he was mad because he hadn't been able to spend the night with Maggie after all, Minta thought cynically. Perhaps they'd even had a row.

She would very much liked to have phoned Dane to tell him about it, but she didn't have an extension in her room and was afraid of facing her father again if she tried to use the one in the kitchen. Thinking of Dane drew her thoughts back to that brief interlude when they had been alone in the sitting-room. He had been right about being able to do better given the right time and place; the way he had made love to her had been the most devastating experience she had ever had. His hands and lips had set her body on fire, even now her body ached for his touch. Dimly Minta realised that he had a great deal of expertise, which must mean that he'd known a lot of women in the past, but it didn't worry her in the least; in fact she was thankful for it; if it had taught him to be that good a lover then she was all for it. She wondered, if her father hadn't come home, whether Dane would have spent the night with her, here, in her own bed. In her imagination she pictured them together, and her body grew hot as she thought of his hands moving over her. But she knew that even her most vivid imaginings could never approach the magic of reality. Not with Dane.

Her throat dry, hands trembling a little, Minta got ready for bed, opening the drawer to take a last look at the delicate underwear she had bought earlier that day. Her hands gently caressed the soft silk. Soon she would be wearing them for Dane. Then she smiled; but not for very long, if tonight was anything to go by. Dane obviously had a high sexual appetite, and she was more than willing to satisfy it, just as often as he wanted.

Richard Tennant left for work as usual the next morning, so Minta was able to avoid him by simply staying in her room until he had gone. Then she hurried down to the kitchen in case Dane called, although she didn't really expect him to this early. After breakfast she hung around in the kitchen until she annoyed Doyley, who shooed her out of the way, so she went up to change, ready to go out and meet Dane the moment he called her. Then, too impatient to wait any longer, she phoned his hotel, only to be told that he had already left, so she had no choice but to wait until he rang about half an hour later.

'Why didn't you call me before?' she demanded. 'I've been waiting and waiting!'

'Sorry, darling; I had an early appointment in Cambridge. I'm there now. I forgot to tell you after everything that happened last night.'

'I wish Daddy hadn't come back.'

'So do I—definitely! But maybe it's just as well he did. *You* are turning out to be a very sexy young lady, capable of undermining all my good intentions.'

'It isn't your good intentions I'm interested in,' Minta told him saucily.

He gave a rich, masculine laugh. 'I'll remind you of that on Tuesday night.'

Minta caught her breath. 'Oh, Dane!'

'I know.' His voice was full of understanding. 'I feel that way too.'

'After you'd left last night,' she said hesitatingly, 'Daddy and I had rather a row.'

'About me?'

'Yes, I'm afraid so. He tried to warn me off you.'

'Oh, hell! I hoped it wouldn't come to this. I'm so sorry, darling. Was it very bad?'

'No, not really. I just told him that I'd go out with you as often as I liked.'

'You didn't tell him that we're engaged? That we're going to be married?'

'No. Just that we're seeing each other.'

'Good girl,' Dane said approvingly, giving her a warm glow of pleasure. 'I don't want you to have to face that alone. Did your father give any reasons for not wanting you to see me again?'

'He said it was because you were trying to negotiate a

deal with his bank. How's it going, Dane? Have you had any success?'

'Some,' he answered cheerfully. 'The meeting I had this morning went very well.'

'When are you coming back?'

'Right now. I should be back in central London in a couple of hours, so we can have lunch.'

They met at an old restaurant in the City where Dr Johnson had once held court, and where they still served the same traditionally English food. When they had eaten their delicious and filling steak and kidney puddings, Dane said, 'I called the hotel before I left Cambridge. There was a message from your father asking me to see him.'

'Are you going to?' Minta asked apprehensively.

'Yes, but not until Monday. I phoned his secretary and she tried to make me see him today, but I managed to fob her off. Being out of town helped, of course.'

'What do you think he wants?'

Dane shrugged. 'It could well be merely business, but then ... well, as he didn't succeed with you, maybe he thought he'd try to persuade me to keep away.'

'Will you tell him then?'

'Yes, I expect so.' He reached out and covered her hand with his. 'Are you afraid, Minta?'

'Of my father? Or of marriage?'

'Both, I suppose.'

She looked troubled. 'I'm not really afraid of Daddy. I know he's bound to be angry at first, but I think he'll come round. We get on well really and we don't usually row at all, last night was an exception.'

'Minta, the last thing I want to do is come between you and your father,' Dane told her earnestly.

'You're not,' she answered instantly. 'It's Daddy who is trying to come between you and me.'

'My darling girl; I don't deserve that.' He looked at her warmly, his hand tightening on hers. 'But you haven't answered the second part of my question.'

'Am I afraid of marriage? Yes, in a way. I'm apprehensive about leaving England and everyone I know, of going to live in a strange country. But I'll be with you, and beside that nothing else matters.' She smiled. 'And I'm certainly not afraid of you.'

But although she denied it so confidently, Minta was a little afraid of him; afraid of the force of emotion he could arouse in her and the power he had to make or mar her happiness; in awe, too, of his worldly sophistication and self-confidence so that she was afraid he might find her too inexperienced. But those things she kept to herself.

They saw each other again that evening and almost constantly over the weekend. Luckily the cold weather broke and the sun came out again; so that they were able to stroll around Regent's Park, watching the breeze catch the last rich golden leaves of autumn and send them whirling and flying across the grass. They walked arm in arm, wrapped up in warm coats, and stopped often to lean against a tree and kiss, and they talked, or at least Minta mostly talked, telling Dane all about herself.

And they talked of their wedding, agreeing that Dane would tell her father on Monday and, depending on his reaction, they would either get married immediately in a Registrar's office, or have a more formal ceremony a couple of days later, when they hoped her father would attend.

'I wish he wasn't so dead set against you,' Minta said

wistfully. 'Just what is that business deal you're negotiating with the bank?'

Dane hesitated a moment, then said, 'You remember I told you I'd inherited some property in the Canaries? Well, it's near the coast and I want to build a holiday village there, on the time-share principle: that's where people buy a couple of weeks in a villa for perpetuity,' he explained. 'And the management maintain the place and make sure everything is running properly. There wouldn't only be villas, of course, but swimming pools, shops, a golf course and tennis courts; everything you'd need for a holiday.'

'And you want Daddy's bank to finance it for you?'

'Not really.' He smiled at her. 'It's a bit involved. I merely want the bank to act as a sort of guarantor.' He pushed a windblown lock of fair hair off her face. 'Do you realise that you haven't kissed me for over half an hour?' he complained.

Minta laughed and stood on tiptoe to put that right at once.

She managed to avoid her father most of the time, sneaking out of the house when he wasn't around and running up to her room when she finally got home late at night. Once he stopped her and angrily demanded to know where she had been and who with, but Minta took refuge in the sulks and refused to answer. Then he started to give her a lecture on childish behaviour, so she simply turned and walked out of the room, to his furious imprecation of, 'Women!'

Whether or not he knew she was going out with Dane, she wasn't sure; he must certainly suspect it. But there was no way he could know just how far things had gone between them. That, Minta thought apprehensively, he wouldn't find out until Dane told him tomorrow.

On Sunday night they sat in Dane's car parked in the street near her house. 'Let me go with you to see him tomorrow,' Minta begged.

'No.' Dane shook his head decisively. 'If you come to the bank with me it would cause too much speculation about us among your father's staff, and I'm sure neither of you would want that. Better to let me face him alone.'

'He's going to be terribly angry,' Minta warned unhappily.

'Then all the more reason that I should take the brunt of it. I respect your father, but I'm not afraid of him,' he reminded her.

She gave a small smile, her eyes running over his broad shoulders. 'I can't imagine you ever being afraid of anything.'

'I'm afraid of losing you,' he said softly, putting his arm round her and drawing her closer. 'I'm afraid your father might persuade you to wait so that I won't be able to take you back with me.'

'He won't,' Minta said forcefully. 'Nothing and no one will ever make me stop loving you. But I can't help worrying about tomorrow. I don't want to alienate Daddy completely. Perhaps it would be better if you didn't tell him in his office.'

'He has to know, Minta,' Dane insisted gently. 'And it was he who asked me to go to his office, not his home.'

'I know, but . . .'

'Stop worrying.' Leaning forward, he kissed her gently on the end of the nose. 'You said yourself that he's bound to come round.' His lips moved to her eyes. 'He'll be okay once he gets used to the idea.' He moved on down the soft line of her cheek, teased the corner of her mouth. 'He's going to have to let you go some time, darling.' His lips moved over hers lightly, in little exploring kisses, and he spoke against her mouth. 'And think what I can give you, that he can't.'

The way he was kissing her, Minta could think of nothing else. Putting her arms round his neck, she returned his kiss hungrily, leaving him in no doubt that she wanted him. His hands moved over her caressingly, then he gave a groan. 'God, Minta, I think the next two days are going to be the longest of my life. The minutes are going to drag like hours until I can make you mine—really mine.'

'I feel the same. I want you so much. Oh, darling, hold me—hold me close.'

They parted at last, with Dane promising to phone Minta the next afternoon, as soon as he'd seen Richard Tennant. She hardly slept that night, wondering what would happen, feeling, despite Dane's assurances, that she ought to tell her father herself or at least be with Dane when he told him. To try to occupy her mind, she spent the morning shopping for the rest of the clothes she needed, buying herself a new coat and a white woollen long-sleeved dress, cut very simply, and also a pretty hat with flowers and a tiny veil. They cost the earth, but it didn't even occur to Minta that it might be hypocritical to charge them to her father's account.

As the time approached for Dane's interview, she grew more and more restless, unable to sit and read a magazine, or do her nails, hovering by the phone in her father's study, willing it to ring even though she knew it was much too early. Once it did ring, but it was only a friend inviting her to a twenty-first birthday party which she had to refuse, finding it difficult to find an excuse when she couldn't tell the truth. For the first time some inkling came to her of how drastically her life was going to change; she was going to a place where she would be without friends, wouldn't even know anyone or speak the language, so that she would be entirely reliant on Dane the whole time. Or at least until she learnt to speak Spanish. Minta optimistically picked up the Spanish phrase book that she'd bought that morning and looked through it for anything she thought would be useful in her new life, but her eyes kept straying to the phone and it was impossible to concentrate.

It was almost four o'clock before Dane finally rang.

'What happened? What did he say?' Minta demanded anxiously before he had time to speak.

'He wasn't exactly overjoyed.' Dane's voice sounded grim, and Minta's heart sank at least three levels. 'As soon as I walked in the room he more or less ordered me to get out of your life and stay out. So it came as something of a shock to him when I told him we were already engaged. He said all the things that we expected: that we hadn't known each other long enough, that we couldn't possibly be sure of our own minds, that I had no right to even think of taking you to live abroad. I told him, of course, that time wouldn't make any difference and that we wanted to get married straightaway.' Dane paused a moment, as if trying to control his voice. 'I'm afraid he got rather angry then. He ordered me never to see you again and said that I was clearly totally irresponsible. He said some other things, too, that I won't repeat.'

'Oh, Dane, was it very bad?'

'It wasn't pleasant,' he admitted. 'I'm glad you weren't there. Eventually I made him see that we were serious about each other, but I'm afraid he wouldn't accept it. He even accused me of . . .' He broke off abruptly.

'Of what?'

But he wouldn't say. 'Nothing. It doesn't matter. We argued for quite some time, and when he found that he couldn't browbeat me into submitting to him, he said that he wanted to see you and speak to you about it.'

'Well, that's to be expected, I suppose. Oh, darling, I'm sorry he gave you such a hard time.'

He laughed. 'My shoulders are broad enough to take it. And you're *definitely* worth fighting for. But I had to make one concession: I promised your father that I'd let him talk to you alone tonight.' He sounded tired suddenly. 'I didn't want you to have to face him alone, but maybe he'll be more reasonable once he's got over his first anger and sees you tonight. As long as you can stand up to him, darling.'

'I will, don't worry. He's—he's not an unreasonable man, Dane. Once he realises that we love each other, I'm sure he'll be okay.' But although she spoke optimistically, Minta had never provoked this kind of crisis before, and she wasn't at all certain how her father would react.

'I hope so. But you must promise me, Minta, that if things become—difficult you'll phone me, and I'll come over and get you.'

'All right, but I'm sure it won't come to that. Did you tell him we've got a special licence? That we could be married tomorrow?'

'No, I thought it best to give him time to simmer down. He had a violent enough reaction to our engagement.'

'It's probably because I'm an only child,' Minta explained. 'And we've been very close since my mother died. I suppose he feels extra-protective towards me. And perhaps he's hurt that I didn't confide in him.'

'Does he confide the details of his affair with Maggie to you?'

'Well, no.' She felt slightly shocked at the thought.

'Then why should he expect you to tell the details of yours to him?' Dane said curtly. Then his voice grew rueful. 'Sorry, darling, I'm afraid your father got my back up. I'll be thinking of you tonight, when you see him.'

'I know. I was thinking of you this afternoon. When will I see you?'

'Tomorrow. Phone me tonight, if you can. If not, as early as possible tomorrow morning. Then we'll decide what we're going to do. I love you, Minta—always remember that. And remember that I'm here if things get too rough.'

'Okay. I love you, too.'

The time in between Dane's call and her father coming home seemed to stretch in light years. Minta talked to Doyley until it was time for the housekeeper to go home and then set about preparing dinner, but so nervously that she burnt the pastry and made the sauce too thick and had to start again. When she heard the door bang as her father came home at last, she jumped, spilling milk on to Doyley's clean floor. She found a cloth and bent down to mop it up just as her father strode purposefully into the room.

'Minta!'

For a moment he didn't see her until she bobbed up again, which ordinarily would have made him laugh, but one look at his face told her that laughter was the farthest thing from his mind today. 'Hallo. Dinner's ready when you are,' she told him brightly, desperately trying to ease the tension.

It didn't work. 'Fenton came to see me today,' he barked at her. 'He had the temerity to tell me you were engaged to him!'

His tone immediately enraged her, but Minta tried to answer as coolly as she could. 'Let's get it right, shall we? You sent for Dane and ordered him never to see me again.'

'So you've already talked to him. I suppose he came straight here after he'd seen me?'

'No, he didn't. He phoned me. What else would you expect?'

'Is it true? Have you been abysmally stupid enough to promise to marry a man you've only known for a few days? Not that you could possibly call it knowing him in that time,' he added sneeringly,

I know him well enough to know that I loved him within hours of meeting him,' Minta retorted, her temper rising. Then, more reasonably, 'Daddy, I know it seems terribly sudden, but these things happen, they really do. I remember your telling me that you knew you wanted to marry Mummy as soon as you saw her, so you know it's true. Please try to understand,' she pleaded.

'That was different entirely. I had the sense to keep my feelings to myself until your mother and I knew each other a lot better. We also knew each other's parents and background; *and* I had no intention of taking her off to a foreign country, away from all her relations and friends. Good God, Minta!' He turned on her exasperatedly. 'Can't you see that it won't do? You know nothing at all about him. He could be a rank opportunist for all you know.'

'And is he?' asked Minta, striving to keep calm, but her hands balled into tight fists below the level of the table where her father couldn't see them.

He seemed about to make some sharp remark, but bit

it back, even now respecting the confidences told to him as a banker. 'No, not entirely. But he needs to make money. His family . . .' Again he stopped, then changed tactics. 'Has he told you why he wanted to see me?'

'Yes, he said he wants the bank to act as a guarantor for his time-share project.'

'And has he told you anything of his family?'

'No. Except that he has an older brother,' Minta remembered.

'Nothing more?'

'No. Why should he? I'm going to marry him, not his family. Just as he wants to marry me—not you,' she answered impertinently, unable to see that it mattered.

But her rudeness goaded her father into losing his temper. 'I'm not going to let you throw yourself away on someone with an unstable background. He isn't right for you, and if you weren't so infatuated with him you'd realise it.'

'I'm not infatuated with him. I love him and he loves me. We're going to be married and I'm going back to the Canary Islands with him!'

'Not if I know anything about it, you're not!' her father shouted.

'There's nothing you can do about it!' Minta yelled back at him furiously, tears of anger in her eyes. 'This isn't the Middle Ages—I'm over twenty-one and I'll do as I damn well like!'

He caught hold of her arm and noticed her ring, which further enraged him. 'Have you—have you slept with him? Is that what this is all about? Has he dared to seduce you?'

Minta had never been more angry in her life. Rounding on her father, she bit out, 'Did you go to bed with Maggie last night? Are you in love with her?'

'Mind your own damn business!' he answered angrily.

'And you mind yours,' Minta retaliated. 'At least Dane and I want to get married! You're the last person who should try and throw morals at me!'

Richard Tennant's face was white with anger. 'Can't you see what Fenton's done to you? He's made you turn on me—the one person who has the right to protect you from men like him. Give him up, Minta. You don't know what the hell you're doing.'

'Oh, yes, I do. I know exactly what I'm doing. And after today you won't have to bother about me at all, because I'll be married to Dane!' Then she ran up to her room, locking the door before throwing herself on to the bed and bursting into tears.

Some time later her father came up and banged on the door, more or less ordering her to come down and have dinner, but she yelled at him to go away. He tried to reason with her, using a more conciliatory approach, but it was too late; Minta put her hands over her ears, and eventually he gave up and went downstairs again. When he had gone, she went into her bathroom and washed her face, still trembling with emotion, but fully determined on what she was going to do. Taking a couple of suitcases down from the top of the wardrobe, Minta began to pack all the new things that she had bought and as many of her favourite clothes as she could cram into the cases. Then she carefully put the trinkets that had come to her from her mother into her handbag; there were one or two other pieces, really good jewels, that also belonged to her, but they were locked away in the bank so she would have to leave them behind. Then there was nothing to do but sit and wait until her father went to bed so that she could creep out of the house and go to Dane.

She hadn't wanted it this way; she would much rather have had a proper wedding in a church, among her family and friends, and with her father giving her away with his blessing. But there was no way she was going to be parted from Dane, possibly for months, when she had the chance of being with him, not even for a white wedding and everything that went with it. Once or twice she considered phoning Dane so that he could come and get her, but rejected the idea because she wanted her father to know that she had gone to him of her own free will. She thought, too, of leaving him a note, but what was the point? He would know that there was only one place she would have gone; to the man she loved.

The thought of being with Dane alleviated much of the sadness and anger from her quarrel with her father, and Minta settled down to wait as patiently as she could until she heard him go to bed around eleven, then for another half an hour or so to make sure he was asleep. Sometimes he read in bed for a while, but when she peeped out she saw that the corridor was in darkness and there was no bar of light under his door. Loaded up with her luggage, she crept down the stairs as quietly as she could and let herself out of the kitchen door. Her Mini was parked in the square near by, but at first the engine wouldn't start and she had visions of having to go back to the house to phone for a taxi, because she'd never find one cruising around in this quiet neighbourhood so late at night. But she pulled the choke out and pumped the accelerator and eventually the cold engine spluttered into life. Minta gave a sigh of relief, thinking how ridiculous she would have felt if she'd had to lug her cases all the way back again.

The streets weren't too busy and it didn't take her

long to reach the Cumberland. She managed to park in a small space in the hotel car park and left her cases in the car. The receptionist gave her a knowing look when she asked for Dane's room number.

'I'm his fiancée,' Minta told him imperiously, her chin coming up.

He didn't look as if he believed her, but picked up the phone and dialled Dane's number. 'There's a lady here, sir, who claims to be your fiancée.' He listened for a brief moment, then said quickly, 'One moment, sir. Could you give me your fiancée's name?' Then he replaced the receiver and said to her, 'Could I have your name, please madam.'

'It's Tennant. Araminta Tennant.'

The man's manner immediately changed. 'I beg your pardon, madam. Mr Fenton will be right down.'

Minta found herself a seat where she could see the lifts, but she had hardly been there a minute before a lift arrived and Dane hurried out.

'Darling! What happened? Did he . . .' But before he could go on Minta burst into tears again. Immediately he put his arm round her and took her straight back into the lift, holding her head against his shoulder until they were in his room. Then he sat her down and poured her a drink from one of the miniatures in the fridge. 'Here, drink this and then tell me what happened.'

Gulpingly she obeyed him and wiped her eyes. 'I'm sorry, I didn't mean to do that.'

Dane took the glass from her and knelt down beside her, taking her trembling hands in his. 'Did he kick you out?'

'Oh, no, nothing like that. But we had the most terrible row and so I—I decided to leave.'

'Why didn't you send for me? I'd have come for you.'

'No, I wanted to leave of my own free will. I—I wanted to come to you.'

'Darling!' He raised a hand to gently touch her face, to wipe away a last tear. 'Didn't he try to stop you?'

'He doesn't know I'm here. I waited until he'd gone to bed before I left.'

'Don't worry about it any more. We'll be married tomorrow as we planned and then nothing your father· can say or do will hurt you again, because you'll have me there to protect you.'

'Oh, Dane!' Minta leant forward and put her head against his. He put his arms round her and held her, tenderly stroking her hair until she had quietened. Then he stood up. 'You'd better stay here at the hotel tonight; I'll book you a room.'

He moved towards the bedside telephone, but Minta got quickly to her feet. 'You don't really want that, do you?'

Dane looked at her questioningly and she came to stand close to him. 'I told you—*I came to you*. To be with you.' Lifting her hands, she slid them up his collar and around his neck. 'Dane, I love you so much. Please—let me stay with you.'

He drew in his breath sharply and then caught her to him, kissing her greedily, her body moulded against his. 'Minta, sweetheart,' he said thickly, 'there's nothing in this world I want more. But are you sure that this is what *you* want? That you wouldn't rather wait until we're married?'

'Oh, no.' She pressed herself against him, deliberately moving her hips to try and arouse him. 'I want you to love me now. Oh, Dane, please—please love me!'

'All right. If that's what you want.'

Minta raised her head to see him looking down at her with a curiously triumphant expression; curious in that there was also a bitter twist to his mouth. But then she forgot everything else as he kissed her again and then, deliberately and slowly, began to take off her clothes. His hands explored as he did so, touching her teasingly through the thin silk of her delicate underwear until she moaned and wanted to tear them off herself, but then his hands were on her skin, fondling, exploring, driving her mad with desire and anticipation. She sighed sensuously, loving what he was doing to her, but wanting so much more. Her hands moved to the buttons of his shirt, impatient to share, but Dane picked her up and carried her over to the bed, pulling back the covers and laying her on the cool sheets. For a moment he stood looking down at her nakedness, then moved away to turn off the light, leaving only the bedside lamp to illuminate the room. She heard him taking off his clothes, but didn't look until he came to lie beside her. His body was strong and athletic, perfect and beautiful. And he was so big that she was almost afraid of his strength. But coupled with this was a deep, humble gratitude that a man so good-looking, so wonderful, should fall in love with her.

Slowly she reached out a hand to touch him, letting it slide down the length of his body, revelling in the breadth of his shoulders, the hard muscles in his arms, the flat plane of his stomach and the strength of his thighs. He let her explore his body as she wanted for several minutes, but then couldn't stand it any longer and pulled her on top of him, kissing her in a fierce frenzy of passion, then rolling over so that she was pinned to the bed by his weight. Then it was Dane's turn to use his hands and mouth, bringing her to such a heat of excitement that she begged him to love her, moaning with desire. Their bodies locked together as he took her, giving her the fulfilment her body craved, making love to her so expertly that she cried out in a climax of ecstasy, her body arching under his as he, too, reached the heights of pleasure, his triumphant voice echoing hers.

For a while they lay still, just kissing gently, murmuring endearments, but Dane hadn't left her before he wanted her again and made love to her a second time.

It was well into the early hours of the morning before Minta slept, only to be awakened by Dane's kisses, his body once more urgent for love, demanding her hands and lips to gratify and delight him. Then they lay exhausted in each other's arms.

'It's morning,' he said to her. Then, with a low laugh, 'The morning of your wedding day.'

'Mm.' Minta snuggled up to him like a cat who had had a whole bowlful of cream. 'Can't we just stay here?'

He laughed and kissed the tip of her nose. 'No, I have a whole lot of arrangements to make.' He sat up, taking up most of the room in the single bed, and reached for the phone. 'What would you like for breakfast?'

She looked up at him, her heart bursting with love. She took his hand and held it against her face. 'You order for me. All I want to eat is you.' He spoke into the telephone, the order including a bottle of champagne, while Minta separated his fingers, running her tongue along the groove between each one.

'Minx!' He put down the phone and looked down at her. 'Are you trying to turn me on again?'

'Of course.' She pushed herself up in the bed and

began to kiss his chest, her tongue circling, tasting, while her left hand explored the other side of his chest, touching him as he had touched her breasts during the night.

Dane gasped and caught her hand, pulled her up beside him and then on to his lap. 'Minta,' he groaned. 'If you knew what that did to me . . .'

Minta laughed. 'I think I'm in a position to know exactly what it does to you. Now I know how to turn you on any time I want to.'

'I can see I'm going to have trouble with you.' His eyes went over her, exploring in the daylight. 'The men in the Canary Islands don't allow female insubordination, you know. They have ways of dealing with their women.'

'Do they?' Minta asked breathlessly. 'What ways?' She moved on his lap, knowing that, even after so many times last night, he already desired her again.

'They beat them regularly every week.' He began to fondle her breasts, watching the sensitive nipples harden under his expert hands. He bent to kiss her, but they were interrupted in the middle of what could have developed into something new and really interesting by a sharp rap on the door.

'Hell!' Dane swore. 'That must be breakfast already.'

'Wait! Don't let them in yet.' Minta ran for the bathroom as he laughed and reached for his white bathrobe.

As her cases were still in the car she had nothing to wear, so she used one of the huge bath sheets to wrap around herself like a Roman toga. She gave the waiter a couple of minutes and then poked her head round the bathroom door. 'Has he gone? Can I . . . Oh!' She stopped with her mouth open in consternation as she saw her father standing by the door.

His staring eyes went from the tumbled bed, the clothes all over the floor, to Dane obviously in just his bathrobe, then to her semi-nakedness. Suddenly he erupted into movement, diving across the room towards her, his hands outstretched, but Dane threw himself in the way while Minta cried out in fear.

'You keep away from her!' Dane shouted.

'Me keep away? It's you! You're not fit to even touch her, let alone . . .' Her father took a swing at Dane's head, but he ducked easily out of the way, catching the older man's arm before he could aim another blow.

'Damn you, let me go! I knew I'd find her here with you. When she wasn't in her room this morning I knew this was where she'd be.'

'If you knew, then why the hell are you making all this fuss?' Dane demanded angrily. 'Where the hell else would you expect her to go after the way you treated her?'

Her father seemed to suddenly collapse and sink into a chair, his head in his hands, his face very white. Frightened that he might be ill, Minta went to go to him, but Dane said curtly, 'Get your things and go and get dressed. I'll handle him.'

'But he might be ill!'

'No, he's all right. And seeing you like that only makes it worse. Go on, do as I say.'

She moved to obey him, picking up her clothes from where they lay scattered on the floor. Then she gave one more scared look at the older man before hurrying into the bathroom, to shower and dress as quickly as she could.

When she came out her father seemed to have recovered a little. He had a drink in his hands and his face was a more normal colour. Dane had managed to dress as far as his shirt and trousers and the breakfast tray was on a table by the window, the bottle of champagne in the ice bucket beside it. At sight of Minta some of her father's anger returned. Swallowing down his drink, he banged down the glass and got to his feet. 'I want to talk to you—alone.'

'Oh, Dad, please. What good would it do?' Minta protested in distress. She moved to Dane's side and took his hand. 'I told you—I love Dane and we're going to be married. Today.'

'That's impossible,' Richard Tennant said sneeringly. 'You can't possibly be married that quickly.'

'Yes, we can.' Dane released her hand and put a protective arm round her shoulders. 'We got a special licence last week and the ceremony is already booked for this afternoon.'

'You got a licence last week? When you'd only just met her? My God, you didn't waste any time, you shameless bastard! Have you no scruples? Does it mean nothing to you, to use the emotions of an innocent girl to get what you want?'

Minta gazed at her father in appalled horror. Dane had gone very white beneath his tan and the hand that held her arm tightened until it hurt, but he didn't say anything; it was she who cried out. 'How *dare* you speak to him like that? How dare you?'

'Because it's true,' her father thundered. 'How can you possibly be so gullible as to believe that he's fallen for you? I tell you he's just using you to get at me—to make me give him the backing he wants.'

'My business with your bank has nothing to do with this,' Dane snapped back angrily. 'And only the most unfeeling of parents would have suggested such a thing in front of Minta.'

'All right, let's call your bluff.' Richard Tennant glared at the younger man, his face dark with hate and anger. 'I'll give you what you want: my bank to stand as guarantor for your impossible scheme and in return you give up Minta and promise never to see or contact her again. Now, you lying young swine, what do you say to that?'

For a second Dane didn't answer and Minta looked quickly up at him. There were two bright patches of colour in his cheeks and he seemed to be finding it difficult to speak. Then, through gritted teeth, *'Get out of here.* Get out before I forget who you are and how old you are and throw you out!'

'You can stop play-acting, Fenton. You've won your dirty game, I tell you. I'll give you my promise in writing here and now, and then we can go back to the bank together and get the agreement properly drawn up.'

Dane took an infuriated step towards him, Minta clinging to his arm. 'Can't you get it into your head?' he shouted. 'You can keep your backing; I'll find it somewhere else. It's Minta I want. She's mine now,' And, as if to emphasise his point, he pulled her roughly to him and kissed her possessively on the mouth, his hand covering her breast.

'You filthy swine! Get away from her!'

Richard Tennant lunged forward, but Minta hastily stepped between them. 'No!' she cried out, so fiercely that it brought her father up short. '*You* go away. I'm not going to let you try and dirty and destroy what's between us any longer. We've told you over and over again that we love each other, but you're so wrapped round by corruption that you won't even listen, let alone believe us. Well, I've had as much as I can stand, now and for ever. Just get out of here. Take your mistrust and your prejudice and get out of my life. I never want to see you again! Do you hear me? I never want to see you again!'

Her voice rose on a hysterical note. Her father stared at her, unable to believe his ears. He reached out a shaking, beseeching hand towards her. Minta looked into his face, then very deliberately turned her back on him, moving into Dane's arms. There was a long, shattering silence in which nobody moved, then her father gave a strangled cry and the door slammed shut behind him.

They were married late that afternoon in a civil ceremony in a Registrar's office not too far from the hotel. Minta wore her white dress and the pretty hat and tried very hard to put the quarrel with her father out of her mind, but she didn't really succeed until Dane put a ring on her finger and smiled down into her eyes as they were declared man and wife. Now she belonged to him, was really his. The ecstasy they had shared last night would be theirs for ever. Her hand shook slightly in his and Dane's grip tightened, giving her strength and comfort. It was cold outside and Minta huddled into her coat, the collar turned up against the wind, until Dane grabbed a taxi to take them to the restaurant where he had booked a table. They lingered over the meal, drank a lot of champagne, and danced afterwards, but it was still early when they left to go back to Dane's hotel. He had told the management to change his room and now they were shown up to one with a large double bed. A fresh bottle of champagne to replace the one they had neither of them felt like drinking that morning stood waiting for them, cool in its bucket of ice. Dane opened it and they drank. Minta felt as if she was in a dream, floating on bubbles of champagne. The angry defiance against her father that had carried her through the day left her now and for a few moments she felt an overwhelming sadness that things had turned out this way, but then Dane saw the lost look in her eyes, took her in his arms and began to kiss her, so that she forgot everything except the fierce desire he aroused in her. Her body craved for his, for the fulfilment he could give her, and beside that nothing else mattered.

Tonight he didn't undress her but let her come to him in the sheer white nightdress, her fair hair falling loosely to the delicate lace. Even though they had made love the night before, it still felt strange to get into bed together, to know that it was now legal for them to do so, that a few words spoken before an official had made it a duty instead of a sin. Perhaps Dane felt it, too, because for a while he was content to just hold her, kissing and stroking her gently, until desire took over and he made love to her with a forceful passion that held more than a hint of possessiveness; as if he was proving to her and the world that she was his, to handle as he pleased. And Minta more than met him halfway, grateful to be taught what would please him and glorying in the satiating pleasure it gave them both.

For a few seconds, when she woke, she couldn't remember where she was. Her throat felt dry and her body tender. But then the reasons for these things came flooding back and she turned eagerly to look at the man beside her. He was still asleep, his features only just discernible in the light that filtered through the drawn curtains. My husband, she thought. My husband—repeating the words and thinking of all that they implied. She would have liked to reach out and touch him but was afraid of waking him, wanting to savour these minutes when she could look at him at her will, much as he must have studied her yesterday morning before he had kissed her into wakefulness. He looked younger when he was asleep, the strong thrust of his jaw relaxed, his mouth softened and not set into a determined line. One dark lock had fallen forward on to his forehead and his lashes fanned his cheeks. It came to Minta that it was the face of a man who was not naturally hard, but who had had to learn to be strong and tough. She knew so little about him really, hardly anything about his past. But there was time, plenty of time. She snuggled up to him, and in his sleep he put his arm round her, holding her against the warmth of his body, murmuring some inaudible words. She smiled contentedly and fell asleep again, secure in his arms.

The telephone ringing almost in her ear woke her the second time. Dane reached across her and picked up the receiver, apparently instantly awake. 'Hallo.' He listened for a second. 'Just a minute.' He covered the mouthpiece, then turned and gave her a light kiss on the nose. 'It's business. Why don't you go and have a bath while I deal with it? Then we'll have breakfast and go out and make arrangements to leave for the Canaries.'

'Okay.' Minta found her nightdress on the floor where Dane had tossed it aside the night before, the delicate lace at the front torn a little by his impatient fingers. There didn't seem to be much point in putting it on. She went to move past him, but he caught her wrist and pulled her towards him, his head level with her breasts. Deliberately he kissed them both until the pink nipples hardened in his mouth. Minta gasped and moaned, her fingers twisting in his hair. 'Dane! Oh, yes—*yes!*'

But he took his head away, smiled at the open sensuality in her face, and gave her a gentle pat towards the bathroom. 'Later,' he murmured.

Going into the bathroom, Minta shut the door behind her and stared at herself in the long mirror. She had delicate skin and there were many small bruise marks on her body, bruises the size of a man's fingers. Her nipples were still hard and she put up a hand to touch them, wondering at their sensitivity, that her body could respond so instantly to Dane's caresses. It was wicked of him to have done it when he had the phone in his hand; he had uncovered the mouthpiece when he had grabbed her and whoever was on the end of the line must have heard her moans and have realised what was going on. The thought that a stranger had heard them was embarrassing but at the same time strangely erotic; she must remember to ask Dane who it was—not that she wanted to meet the person, that *would* be embarrassing.

She sang happily as she bathed; Dane came in and offered to wash her back for her, but then he moved on to her front, and what followed drove all memory of asking him who was on the phone completely from her mind.

Eventually they sat down to an extremely belated breakfast, during which Dane told her that he had got to go out on business. 'Sorry, darling, but there's no way I can avoid it.'

'Oh, no, must you really? I shall be so bored here alone. Who is it you have to see?'

'Just someone I contacted last week. It's to do with the time-share scheme, so I must see him. But you don't have to stay here; why don't you go and fix up our flight to the Canaries tomorrow? Then I'll meet you and we'll take in a film or something. And I expect you'll need to buy some more summery clothes; it's much warmer than here, remember.'

Minta smiled, having already packed for a warmer climate, but she spent the next few hours on her own quite contentedly, often pausing to sneak glances at herself in mirrors and shop windows, trying to see if she looked any different now that she was married, her eyes admiring the rings that shone on her left hand. In fact she did look different; love and fulfilment had brought a radiance to her face that showed in the bloom of her skin, the delicate flush in her cheeks and above all in the happiness that shone from her eyes. She was by no means a plain girl, but it had taken love to make her beautiful. From time to time that happiness was shadowed by remembrance of the quarrel with her father, but she still felt so resentful of the way he had spoken to Dane that anger soon took its place.

They met as they had planned and went on to the cinema. Minta asked Dane how his meeting had gone, but he returned a noncommittal answer and she didn't push it, too wrapped up in their new relationship to be really interested in anything else.

When they got back to the hotel and went up to their room she was amazed to find several boxes and suitcases which, when she opened them, contained the rest of the clothes she had left behind at home and her more treasured possessions that she hadn't had room to pack. Dane silently crossed to the phone and rang down to reception. He talked for a few minutes, then put the phone down and turned to her. 'They were sent round earlier this afternoon. There was no message with them. It seems as if your father has decided to cut you out of his life!'

They spent that night at the hotel and left for Gran
Canaria early the next morning. Minta made no
attempt to get in touch with her father. If he could cut
her out of his life then she could certainly do the same
to him!

CHAPTER FOUR

THE warm clothes that Minta had worn to keep out the early morning cold of London seemed superfluous as soon as she stepped off the plane. The sun was shining and there wasn't even a breeze to detract from the warmth of the day.

'Is it summer here?' she asked in surprise, lifting her face to the sun.

'No, but the climate's more or less the same here the whole year round, it only varies by about fifteen degrees the whole time.'

'Lovely! I'll be able to get a tan straightaway, then.'

Dane's car was in the airport car park where he had left it two weeks ago. Two weeks in which their lives had completely changed. He drove straight to the capital of the island, Las Palmas. It was only during the flight over that it had occurred to Minta to wonder where they were going to live, and she had been disappointed when Dane told her that they would have to go to a hotel, that the house he owned had been lent to a friend whom he would have to ask to leave before they could move in. She looked around at her new home with interest as they drove along but didn't like the grey, barren hills and flat, treeless plains. 'Why aren't there any trees?' she demanded.

'The islands are volcanic and this area got covered by lava years ago. The main agricultural areas are farther north.'

'The volcanoes are extinct, aren't they?' Minta asked in some alarm.

Dane laughed. 'You don't have to worry, they haven't been active for a hundred years or so.'

They came to the outskirts of Las Palmas, a large sprawling town that was built along the narrow neck of a thin peninsula of land, the coastlines forming a busy shipping port on one side and tourists' resort on the other. The hills overlooking the town were built on, to what seemed impossible heights, by block after block of apartment buildings, all painted a dingy grey-white and very barrack-like. There was a good road in from the airport, an *autopista*, Dane called it, but once they turned off this the streets were clogged with cars closely packed on either side, leaving hardly space for two cars to pass each other.

'Good heavens,' Minta exclaimed. 'I thought parking in London was bad enough, but this is crazy!'

Steering carefully round a car that was parked right on a corner, Dane said, 'Yes, there's no point in having a decent car here; you can almost guarantee that it will get scratched or dented however carefully you drive.'

He drew into the forecourt of a large hotel, the Reina Isabel, which backed on to the long, golden stretch of Las Canteras beach. They were given a room on the second floor with a private bathroom, and Minta wasted no time in changing into something cooler. 'Aren't you going to change?' she asked Dane. 'You must be baking in that woollen suit.'

'I only took winter clothes with me to London. All my lightweight stuff is in my—my flat.'

Minta's forehead creased into a frown. 'Why couldn't we go there instead of staying at a hotel?'

'It's much too small. It's really just a couple of rooms at the back of my office in the town. Not at all suitable for you.' He came over and put his hands on her arms, kissed her on the forehead. 'If you're ready, why don't we go down to the restaurant and have lunch? I hate that pre-packaged stuff they give you on planes. Then you can unpack while I go and collect my clothes and bring them over.'

'Can't I come with you?'

'Better not. I must go into the office and make sure the instructions I sent from England are being carried out. There's a lot to do, I'm afraid,' he told her ruefully.

Minta's hazel eyes filled with disappointment. 'Oh, but I—I thought we would have a honeymoon.'

'And we will—just as soon as I can manage it. But I'm afraid you'll have to be patient for a while, darling. I hadn't anticipated bringing a bride back with me from London, and just now there's so much to do to get the time-share project off the ground.'

'Couldn't you postpone it—just for a week?'

He shook his head regretfully. 'No. But I'll make it up to you, I promise. You'll have the best belated honeymoon anyone ever had. And I'll try to be with you as much as possible.'

And with that she had to try to be satisfied; and the fact that she had lived with her father since she had left school helped because she understood how important a man's work and business was to him, but she couldn't help wishing that it could be otherwise.

When Dane left her after lunch, Minta went out on to the beach and walked along at the water's edge, the sun on her back. There were lots of tourists sprawled out on loungers in neat lines, facing the sun, their skins ranging in all shades from milk white to a dark brown, with here and there the patchy skin of someone who had been too long in the sun in different clothes. But there weren't many like that; the people who could afford to come to the Canaries in November were the kind who had a tan most of the year. She walked back along the wide promenade that parallelled the beach and was lined with restaurants and tourist shops, admiring the hand-embroidered silk blouses and linen tablecloths in the windows. She wondered how much furniture and household stuff there was in Dane's house, and began to imagine how she would arrange and decorate the place, even though she had never seen it. When she got back to the hotel, she went in eagerly, but Dane hadn't yet returned, so she changed into a bikini and left him a note, then went up to the swimming pool on the roof to sunbathe.

Dane found her there an hour or so later, just as Minta was deciding that the warmth had gone out of the sun and it was time to go in. He had changed into a pair of pale blue lightweight slacks and a navy knitted shirt, both of which had good labels. Minta's heart leapt when she saw him walking round the pool, looking for her, and she thought she would burst with pride when two girls near by remarked admiringly on his looks.

'Mmm,' one girl said, nudging the other. 'D'you see what I see? What I wouldn't give for him! I haven't seen him around here before. I wonder if he's with anyone.'

The other girl turned over to look. 'Wow! I see what you mean. I wouldn't exactly turn *him* away from my door on a cold, dark night!'

'Not even if he was a wolf,' the first girl agreed, and they both giggled, their eyes following Dane in frank appraisal as he came nearer.

He walked past them as if they didn't exist and sat down on the edge of Minta's sun-bed, leaning down to kiss her lingeringly. 'Miss me?' he demanded softly.

She decided to tease him. 'Are you back already? The time's gone so quickly I hadn't noticed.'

'You heartless jade. And a bride of only two days as well! I can see what my life's going to be like with you.'

'Can you?' Minta whispered, putting her hands on his shoulders.

'Most definitely,' he answered softly, his lips finding hers again in little kisses. 'And I'm going to enjoy every minute of it.' Then he pulled her to her feet. 'Come and swim.'

'I'm not very good,' Minta said doubtfully. 'And it's getting late.'

But he was already pulling off his shirt and unzipping his trousers. Minta already knew that he had a superb body, but even so she caught her breath when she saw him in the small, tight-fitting swimming trunks that left no one in any doubt as to his manhood. 'Come on, race you in!'

He went to the side and dived in neatly, coming up several yards away and setting off down the pool in a swift, clean crawl, but Minta went timidly up to the shallow end and climbed down the ladder into the heated pool, She didn't swim very well and was more than half afraid of the water.

Dane's head broke the surface nearby. 'Swim down to the deep end.'

'No!' she protested in alarm. 'I told you I'm not very good.'

'Okay. Try and do a width here, then. I'll help you.'

He stayed beside her, encouraging and teaching, for almost half an hour, and by the end of that time Minta was swimming better and enjoying it more than she had ever done before. When they came out he wrapped a big towel round her as she began to shiver, feeling cold out of the warmth of the water now that the sun had gone in.

'You did fine,' he praised. 'Practise every day and you'll soon get really good.' He patted most of the wet off her, his hands lingering where they shouldn't.

'Behave yourself!' Minta admonished, loving every minute of it. 'People are watching.'

'Let them; they're only jealous.' But he gave her the towel and picked up his own. 'I'd better change; towelling *you* dry has the strangest effect on me.'

They went down to their room and Minta went into the bathroom and took off her wet bikini, turning on the shower to let the water run hot. Dane came to stand in the doorway. He was completely naked. 'Want some help?' he asked lazily.

She looked into his eyes and her heart started to race. She nodded wordlessly and he came over and picked her up, holding her high in his arms, his lips kissing hers and then moving on down the length of her body. Then he gently carried her into the shower and stood her on her feet while he began to soap her all over, his hands lingering in all the most erogenous places. Minta's breath caught in her throat, her eyes closing as she lost herself in euphoric delight.

'Don't I get to be washed?' Dane murmured softly in her ear.

She opened heavy-lidded eyes, her lips parted sensuously. Taking the cake of soap from him, she slowly began to soap his shoulders and then work on down. He was holding her by the hips and she could feel his grip gradually tightening as her hands rubbed and stroked, leaving white trails in the lather on his skin. 'Oh, God, Minta!' The words came out on a groan and his fingers bit into her skin. 'Go on. Don't stop— not yet.'

But in the end it was he who made her stop, because he suddenly jerked her up into his arms, carried her out of the bathroom and threw her down on to the bed, then, still covered in soap as they both were, he made love to her in a fervent blaze of passion that lifted her to a vortex of pleasure.

'Oh, Dane,' Minta sighed afterwards, her body satiated. 'That was the best. But every time is the best.' She picked up his hand and kissed it, tasting the soap that lingered there. 'Will it always be as good as this?'

Dane smiled and pushed a lock of hair off her damp brow. 'How young you are!'

Minta pulled away. 'I don't like that,' she complained. 'You make it sound as if being young makes you stupid and naïve.'

'There's nothing wrong with being naïve. I just meant that you're not very experienced.'

'And you are, I suppose,' Minta said with more than a touch of jealousy.

'Enough to know that love changes with time. At the moment sex is the most important part of it, but gradually other things will become as important.'

'Do you mean children?' she asked doubtfully, thinking that nothing could ever be as important as sex.

'Not really; they're only part of it. There are other things.'

'Do you want children?' she asked.

'Of course. Do you?'

'Oh, yes. At least two. I may be pregnant already,' she reminded him.

He put a hand on the soft swell of her stomach. 'So you may. A girl as lovely as you.'

'No, I'd rather have a boy with dark hair and gorgeous grey eyes.' Her voice trailed off as she traced the contours of his face with her finger. 'But on second thoughts,' she added rather huskily, 'I think I'd rather wait before we have a baby. I don't want to be fat and unattractive so that you won't want me. And I don't want to have to share you—not yet.'

'Darling, you'll never be unattractive to me. Don't you know that? But if you really want me to prove it to you all over again . . .'

It was several days before Dane told her that his friend had now left his house and they were free to move in. During that time he had had to leave her on her own for long periods when he was working, and she had spent the time exploring the town, sunbathing, and assiduously practising her swimming because she thought it would please him. She also wrote to several friends and a few relations in England, telling them of her marriage and giving them the hotel address, but she didn't attempt to write to her father. Not only could she not bring herself to forgive him, but the way he had sent her things on after her clearly indicated that he wanted nothing more to do with her. If there was one thing more than any other that Minta had inherited from her father it was obstinacy; they could both be as stubborn as the proverbial mule over an issue, and whereas before it hadn't mattered too much, this time they had clashed head-on, and Minta was darned if she was going to make the first move towards a reconciliation.

When Dane joined her in the evenings they would have drinks in the hotel bar and then go into the restaurant for dinner, afterwards strolling through the narrow streets of the town, mostly down across the narrow strip of land to the Santa Catalina park, which was a large square facing the opposite bay, near the port. The square was an essentially continental place, always thronged with people at any time of day, sitting outside at the open-air cafés, under the shade of palms and enormous Canary laurel trees, watching the stallholders who sold everything from postcards to antiques, and where a bootblack would clean Dane's shoes for just a few pesetas while they sipped their coffee and Minta nibbled delicious roast almonds bought from a man who sold them from a basket.

She hadn't liked the look of the town when she first saw it and there were certainly parts that were extremely ugly, but there was something about the place that got to you, especially here, where there was always something going on, but it was life enjoyed in a leisurely, civilised way, without the fearful rush of mainland cities. Once or twice Minta had walked down to the square on her own for a mid-morning coffee, but Dane warned her never to go there alone in the evening, because it was then that the seamen from the ships in the port came into the town to try to pick up girls. Because the island was so new to her Minta didn't mind being left by herself so much, and there were always the evenings to look forward to, when, after they had had dinner and sat in the square for an hour or so, Dane would raise his eyebrow in a silent question and she would nod eagerly in answer. Then they would walk back to their hotel hand in hand, their bodies close, and make love until they fell into exhausted, satiated sleep.

They checked out of the hotel immediately after breakfast one morning and Dane drove her to their new home, their suitcases filling the boot and the back of the car. It wasn't very far away, set in a small street only a few hundred yards from the Avenida Marítima, the main road that ran along the edge of the sea on the port side of the isthmus. There were double wooden gates set into a high wall overhung with trees, that led into a small paved courtyard just large enough to take the car. To the right of the courtyard was a small but very pretty garden, bright with red poinsettias and purple and orange bougainvillea that trailed along the wall and up the front of the house, mingling in a confused mass with climbing geraniums which grew like weeds in pink and red profusion. There were, too, several trees and shrubs, including two tall palm trees that cast dancing ballerina shadows on the grass, and a lemon tree, its tangy scent carried on the slight breeze from the sea.

Minta turned towards the house and gave an involuntary exclamation of pleasure. It wasn't very large, but what it lacked in size it more than made up for in attractiveness. It was painted white, as were most of the houses on the island, and had a low-pitched roof of rich red pantiles. Double solid wooden doors, painted a dull black, were on the left side of the house with a window further along, but the most attractive feature of the building was a large, ornately carved wooden balcony on the first floor, set under a little roof also hung with pantiles. From this roof and along the ledge of the balcony there stood or hung dozens of pots of geraniums and other flowers so that there was almost a miniature garden up there.

'Oh, how lovely! It's gorgeous,' Minta enthused, her eyes alight with pleasure.

'I hope you'll like it as much inside,' Dane remarked. 'The house used to belong to my grandmother's family and is rather old, but I've had central heating put in and the kitchen modernised.'

'I'm going to love it—I just know I am!' Minta flung

her arms round his neck and kissed him exuberantly, overflowing with happiness.

He unlocked the double doors and she moved to walk eagerly in ahead of him, but Dane held her back. 'Oh no; we do it this way.' And he stooped to pick her up in his arms and carry her over the threshold into the cool, dim interior.

Minta laughed with delight and kept her arms round his neck when he set her on her feet, looking up into his face, her own suddenly serious. 'Thank you,' she said earnestly. 'Thank you so very, very much.'

'For what?' Dane smiled down at her.

'For this house. For being so wonderful. For loving me.'

The smile faded and he frowned. 'Don't sell yourself short,' he told her, his voice rough. 'It isn't all one-sided.'

'No. No, of course not,' Minta agreed uncertainly, taken aback by his change of mood. Taking her arms down, she caught hold of his hand and said brightly, 'Come and show me over the house.'

He did so willingly enough. On the ground floor there was a large sitting-room looking out over the garden, furnished comfortably in a happy mixture of rather heavy Spanish antique pieces with a bright new three-piece suite, a music centre with loads of records, and a bookcase crammed full of modern novels. There was also a small dining-room, an even smaller room that Dane said was used as a study, and a kitchen. On the upper floor there were two bedrooms and a bathroom opening off a corridor which ended in that divine balcony overlooking the garden. All the rooms had tiled floors and plain white walls, but there were rich rugs and lots of pictures to take away any feeling of bareness.

'It's heavenly!' Minta exclaimed excitedly. 'Shall we have this bedroom?' She indicated the one overlooking the garden.

'Of course. It has the biggest bed.'

'And we'll make great use of it, won't we?'

'Indeed we will,' he promised. 'Starting tonight. But now I'm afraid I must go. I have to drive down to the site of the time-share development to meet the architects. You'll be all right here unpacking, won't you?'

'Yes, of course. But what about dinner?'

'We'll eat out.'

'Hey! I am a Cordon Bleu cook, you know. I can quite easily go out and get something and cook it here.'

'But will you be able to ask for what you want in the shops? I'll have to find someone to give you Spanish lessons now that we've moved in here,' he said, half to himself. 'Anyway, I'll leave it to you. But if you do go out take a taxi; I don't want you getting lost.' He gave a glance at his watch. 'I *must* go, or I shall be late. 'Bye, darling.' He went to give her a quick kiss, but Minta grabbed him round the waist and kissed him properly, moving her hips voluptuously against him in a way that she had already learnt excited him almost beyond control.

'Hey, what are you trying to do?' he demanded as soon as he could breathe. 'Put me down, woman!'

But Minta had already pulled his shirt out of his trousers and her hands were at his belt. 'Not until we've tried that bed out,' she told him mischievously, and pushed him backwards so that he fell across it.

'There isn't time; I have to be at the site by . . .' His words trailed off as Minta's hands, more practised now, roused and inflamed his sexual appetite. 'God,' he groaned, pulling her on top of him. 'A man could go bankrupt with a sex-cat like you around!'

When he finally left, at least half an hour late, Minta purred like the sex-cat he had called her. Lying there on the ruffled covers of the big bed, she revelled in her own happiness, thanking all the gods for letting her meet and fall in love with Dane and for the sexual joy and fulfilment he had given her. He was such a sensational lover—she was sure there couldn't be another couple in the world as happy as they were. She spent a delightful day exploring the house and garden, unpacking their cases and stowing all the things away in the empty wardrobes and chests of drawers in the bedroom. The top drawer she chose for her own things, and as she laid her underwear in it she felt something lumpy under the paper that lined the old wood. Fishing it out, she was astonished to find a woman's earring. It was rather an ornate piece of jewellery, the type for pierced ears, and set with red and white stones that sparkled in the sun coming in from the garden. Taking it over to the window for a closer look, she was even more surprised to see that the stones were real, which must make it quite valuable. Whoever had lost it must surely have missed it, but they obviously hadn't searched in the right place.

With a shrug, Minta dropped the earring into a little dish on the top of the dresser and forgot about it until she noticed it that evening as they were changing to go out to dinner. Dane had come home late and they had decided to eat out. 'Hey, your friend that you lent the house to—did he have a girl-friend?' she called out to Dane who was in the bathroom.

'Why do you ask?' He stood in the doorway, a towel in his hands.

'Because I found an earring under the lining of one of the drawers in the dresser this morning.' She laughed. 'Unless your friend liked to dress up in women's gear!'

'No, of course not.' Dane came over and looked at the piece of jewellery in her outstretched hand. 'I suppose he must have had a girl here. I'll see that he gets it back.'

'Who is your friend? Are you going to introduce me to him?'

'No.' The word came out curtly and Minta's brows arched in surprise. Seeing it, Dane gave a shrug and a small smile, saying, 'That is, I can't introduce you because he's gone over to Tenerife to live. He couldn't find anywhere else in Las Palmas.'

'That's a shame. I haven't met any of your friends yet.'

'No—well, I've been too busy to make many friends since I've been here. Most of the people I know are business acquaintances, and they're nearly all Canarios and don't speak much English.' He turned away and began to dress.

'I thought you'd lived here a long time?'

'Only as a child when my grandmother was alive. We came for a few holidays after she died, but that was all.'

'And your brother—doesn't he live in the Islands?'

'No, he lives in England all the time now.'

Minta's brow wrinkled in puzzlement. 'Why didn't you invite him to our wedding, then? He could have been your best man.' Dane stood with his back to her, looking for a tie, and didn't answer. '*He* didn't object to you marrying me, did he?' she asked, half joking, half uncertain.

Dane straightened up. 'It didn't matter whether he was there or not. You were all that mattered to me.

Why don't you come over here and tie this tie for me,' he added, 'instead of sitting there throwing questions at me.'

She gave a gurgle of laughter and came to do as he asked, her tongue between her teeth as she concentrated. Something in his tone had told her that Dane didn't want to pursue the subject, but being a woman she perversely said, 'You have told your brother that we're married, haven't you?'

His hand closed over hers in a sudden, vice-like grip. 'He had a nervous breakdown,' he said grimly. 'He isn't in a fit state to care one way or the other.'

'Oh, I *am* sorry. Is it very bad?'

'Yes.'

And now, too late, Minta left the subject alone. As she looked round for some new topic, her eyes settled on the earring and she picked it up again. 'I wonder who your friend's girl-friend was. She must be pretty wealthy if she could afford to lose an earring like this; these stones are real.'

'I've already said I'd see to it,' Dane said harshly, taking the earring from her and dropping it into his pocket. 'For God's sake let's forget about it and go out and eat.'

Then he strode out of the room leaving Minta staring after him in consternation, wondering what on earth she had done to upset him.

That night, for the first time, Dane didn't make love to her. Minta lay beside him listening to the even sounds of his breathing, the moonlight from the unshuttered windows lying across the counterpane. She felt terribly lonely and sort of empty inside, needing the reassurance of his touch, his nearness. He had been rather abstracted all evening and, although she had done her best to be bright and amusing, she hadn't been able to completely break down the barrier that he had withdrawn behind. She had suggested that they come straight home after their meal instead of going for a walk along the promenade, hoping that they would make love and she would be able to get through to him that way. But, although she had been quite wanton in her efforts to arouse him, Dane had merely caught her exploring hands, kissed her gently, and turned off the light, falling almost immediately asleep.

And now she lay trying to work out what she had done to make him act like this, realising that it could only be talking about his brother that had upset him. The illness of a close relative must, of course, be upsetting to anyone, and Dane must obviously care very deeply about his brother to not even want to talk about it, especially to her. Minta longed to share his hurt with him, to comfort him; that was what love meant, wasn't it—to share the good and the bad? Raising herself on her elbow, she looked down at his sleeping face, outlined in the moonlight. How quickly he had become indispensable to her life. If anything happened to him she wouldn't want to go on living. It distressed her greatly that she had inadvertently hurt him, that was the last thing she ever wanted to do. Especially, she admitted honestly to herself, if it meant that he didn't want to make love, even for a night. Until she had met Dane she had never realised how wonderful sex could be, but he had aroused a sexual appetite in her that needed to be constantly appeased. She decided that first thing tomorrow morning she would apologise for upsetting him, tell him that she didn't want to pry, but that she loved him, and that if any time he felt like talking about it she was there, waiting to listen and help if she could.

But as it turned out, Minta never said any of those things, because as she came languorously awake the next morning, she felt Dane's hands on her, softly stroking her warm skin. As happened every night when she wore a nightdress, it had rumpled upwards while she slept and ended up gathered around her waist. She was lying on her front, her legs sprawled apart, and for a few minutes she stayed that way, pretending to be still asleep, revelling in the intoxicating touch of his hands. But then his probing fingers made her gasp and she turned over to face him, her eyes alight with ardent expectation. He had pulled back the covers and was leaning over her quite naked, his body lit by the glow of the morning sun. Reaching up, he helped her to take off the nightdress and then kissed her gently on the mouth, his hands caressing her breasts into wakefulness, to be closely followed by his lips and his tongue, going on down her body, fondling each other, each valley, his seductive lips lighting a fire inside her that burned to a white heat.

'Oh, Dane! *Now!* Make love to me *now*,' she begged, her voice panting as she moved against his hands, her cheeks flushed with heat and a film of perspiration on her skin.

But still he held back, his mouth and fingers driving her so wild that she finally grabbed hold of him by the arms and pulled him up on top of her. Dane put an arm under her hips and lifted her towards him, making love to her so forcefully that he sent wave after wave of ecstasy coursing through her body, her senses lost in a whirlpool of pleasure in which she could feel nothing but the wonderful, wonderful sensations in her own body. She cried out his name aloud, her fingers digging into his shoulders, knowing that he was sharing her rapture.

When it was over, Minta didn't move for a long time, she just lay there, her breathing gradually returning to normal, and didn't even open her eyes until she felt Dane get off the bed. He stood looking down at her, his eyes slowly running over her body, seeing the marks of his lovemaking: the lethargy in her limbs, the radiant satiation in her face. He smiled, 'Go back to sleep,' and pulled the thin sheet up over her.

Minta lifted her arms towards him and he bent to kiss her. 'Will you come home at lunchtime?'

'For a siesta?' he asked, his eyebrows rising.

'Why not?' She smoothed the sheet down over her slim figure, hoping the gesture would intrigue him.

And it did. 'I'll try,' he answered. 'It depends how things work out.' He grinned. 'Keep it hot for me if I can't!' And he wasn't talking about lunch.

Minta lay back on her pillow, supremely content, as she listened to Dane shower and dress. How stupid she had been to suppose that he had been annoyed with her last night; perhaps he had just been tired—after all, he had a right to be, working hard with his time-share project and conducting a sex-filled honeymoon at the same time! Minta chuckled to herself. But he certainly hadn't been tired this morning, and he had more than made up for last night. She curled herself into a ball like a contented cat in the sun and fell asleep again before Dane came over to say goodbye.

Later that morning she ventured out to shop for the first time, determined to cook herself that evening so that they could have a candlelit dinner at home. The menu had been easy to work out and she had the list of ingredients she needed in her bag, plus her Spanish phrase book, but she had an idea that she would have to rely heavily on sign language and pointing at things.

The largest department store in Las Palmas is El Corte Inglés, a huge building that takes up a whole triangular-shaped block in a road that runs at right angles to the harbour. Minta thought she would go there first to buy candles as she hadn't been able to find any whole ones in the house, and as it was such a lovely morning, in more ways than one, she decided to walk, knowing that as long as she kept the sea on her right she would eventually get to where she wanted to go.

As she set off, dressed in a cool summer dress, a shopping basket over her arm, she didn't notice a woman sitting in a parked car on the other side of the street, nor that it overtook her once she had turned into the main road, then stopped and waited again until she had passed, afterwards driving into the underground car park beneath the department store when the watcher saw that that was her destination.

There were lots of beautiful things in the store that Minta would have liked to linger over, but there would be plenty of time for that in the future. She concentrated on buying her candles and one or two cooking utensils that she needed. These things were easy enough as all she had to do was pick the things up and carry them to the cash desk, but then, as she was going down the escalator, her eye was caught by a male model wearing a beautiful cashmere sweater which would look perfect on Dane and would be ideal for the cooler evenings. Succumbing to temptation, she found an assistant and tried to explain what she thought Dane's English size was, and that she wanted to take the sweater for him to try but bring it back and change it if it didn't fit. The assistant, however, didn't speak any English, so he went to find a colleague who could, but he was little better, and somehow they got into a hopeless muddle.

'Perhaps I can help?' a pleasant English voice interrupted just as Minta was beginning to think of giving up the whole idea. Turning, she saw a tall, slim, dark-haired girl standing near by, looking at her in tentative interrogation. The girl looked to be a few years older than herself, had a glorious tan and looked and spoke with the ease that comes from sophistication and attractiveness. Minta felt a stab of jealousy; she had always longed to be tall and sophisticated. But the girl was saying, 'You seem to be having some difficulty with the language, and I do speak Spanish . . .'

'Thank you,' Minta's flash of jealousy was instantly lost in gratitude. 'I'm trying to buy this sweater for my husband, but I'm not sure of these foreign sizes.'

The girl smiled and turned to the assistant, her Spanish fluent and impeccable, and in no time at all the problem had been sorted out and the sweater wrapped and paid for. Her rescuer laughed and waved away Minta's thanks. 'It was no bother. Are you on holiday here?'

'No, I live here. Or at least I've just come to live here, and I'm afraid I don't speak any Spanish yet. You speak the language so well; I suppose you're a Canary Islander?'

The girl shook her head. 'No, I'm as English as you are, but I used to be a travel courier so I learnt to speak it quite well. Then I fell in love with the islands and decided to settle here.' She smiled. 'Have you got much more shopping to do? Perhaps I can translate for you.'

'That's very kind of you, but I'm sure you must have things of your own you want to do,' Minta demurred.

'No, as a matter of fact I was just killing time, and it's great to meet an English girl of my own generation who actually lives here. So if I can help. . . .'

Minta accepted gratefully. 'Well, thanks. I do have rather a long list.'

'Show me.' Minta passed over her list and the girl said, 'Oh, what you need is the local market. I've got my car here; I'll drive you. It isn't all that far, but it's difficult to find.'

So Minta found herself being driven along by her new acquaintance, who introduced herself as Delia Nelson. She seemed interested and friendly, and Minta was soon confiding that she had recently married and her husband had brought her here to live. The market was a local one, busy and colourful, where it was necessary to feel and prod and bargain for what you wanted. Delia seemed completely at home there and Minta's basket was soon full of all the fruit and vegetables she needed, plus some that she had never heard of before and wanted to experiment with. From the market, Delia drove to a supermarket in Las Palmas where Minta got the rest of the things she needed.

'There.' Delia crossed the last item off the list. 'That's everything. I enjoyed that. What are you going to make?' Then, when Minta told her, 'Mm, that sounds delicious. You must be a super cook.'

'You must come to lunch some time and find out,' Minta offered with a laugh.

'Thanks, I'd like that. Now, you'd better let me drive you home. Where do you live?'

'Oh, but I can't take up any more of your time.'

'Nonsense, you'll never be able to carry all this lot. What's your address?'

Minta told her, glad of the lift, because she had gone a bit mad in the market, buying quite a lot more than she had intended because all the goods had looked so colourful and tempting and because she wasn't used to buying in kilos instead of pounds. When they got to the house, she felt that the least she could do was to ask Delia in for a coffee.

'Oh, how delightful!' the other girl exclaimed when she saw the house. 'You *are* lucky. I have to make do with a flat that looks on to the roof of the building across the street where a man keeps all his pigeons. What a lovely balcony. May we have our coffee up there?'

'Yes, of course. Come on in.'

The two girls were soon sitting in the shade of the balcony, Minta sitting with her back to the road, looking out over the garden, her guest opposite her. They found many things to talk about, Delia giving her the name of a good hairdresser and telling her where to find a library that had a selection of English books. The time passed unknowingly quickly as they sat there; Minta only now realising how much she missed having someone of her own sex and age to talk to since she had met Dane. Dane was quite perfect, of course, but there were some things you just couldn't share with a man, like clothes and make-up and the purely feminine topics. But despite her enjoyment, she eventually realised that it must be almost lunchtime, and she wished that Delia would go in case Dane came home; she didn't want to waste a minute of the time when she would be alone with him. But the other girl seemed in no hurry to go, her eyes often looking past Minta to the road as she talked. But then, just as Minta was on the point of having to ask her to go, Delia broke off what she was saying and got to her feet. 'Good heavens, is that the time? I'm so sorry, I had no idea. It's been such an enjoyable morning. Perhaps you'll come and have coffee with me one day? Here, I'll write down my address and telephone number.' Taking a piece of paper from her bag, she wrote on it and passed it over.

Minta stuffed the paper in the pocket of her dress and escorted Delia outside. She was just going to open the gate to let her out, when Delia exclaimed, 'Oh, my sunglasses! I must have left them in your sitting-room, or perhaps on the balcony.'

She moved to go in search of them, but Minta said, 'I'll find them for you,' and ran indoors.

They weren't in the sitting-room, so Minta went up to the balcony. As she reached it she glanced out over the garden wall and saw that Dane had come home, leaving his car in the road and walking up to the gate. She looked round for Delia's glasses, unable to find them at first, then spotted them on the floor behind the chair where she had been sitting. She stooped down to pick them up just as Dane came through the gate. Bother, now he would find a complete stranger in the garden with no one to introduce him.

'What the hell are *you* doing here?' Dane's thunderstruck voice carried to her quite clearly as she went down on her knees to reach the glasses. 'You promised to keep away!'

'I know, Dane darling, but I just had to come.'

Minta peered through the foliage of the plants on the balcony and saw Delia Nelson run into her husband's arms!

CHAPTER FIVE

Too stunned to believe her own eyes, Minta stared down at the couple in the garden, but then Dane looked towards the house, and she quickly ducked down beneath the shelter of the balcony again, the action completely involuntary.

'Where is she?' Dane's sharp tone carried to her quite clearly.

'Inside.'

He lowered his voice but still spoke urgently. 'Why did you come here? You could ruin everything for me.'

'I couldn't find one of the earrings you gave to me. I was afraid I'd left it behind here and she might find it. You made me pack so quickly—first your things and then mine . . .'

'She found it yesterday, but I managed to pass it off. I've been trying to contact you all morning to tell you.'

Up in her hiding-place, Minta's blood ran cold in her veins and she began to shiver despite the sun. It couldn't be true. Oh God, please don't let it be true! She wanted to stand up and scream, but she stayed where she was, listening, her ears straining to catch every word.

'Does she know who you are? My God, you haven't told her?'

'No, of course not.' Delia's voice was quick to reassure him. 'I followed her to the shops and pretended to meet her by accident. She doesn't suspect a thing.'

Liar! Minta thought agonisingly. You know I'm here. You set this up so that I would find out.

'You'd better get out of here before she comes back.' Dane's voice faded a little and Minta could imagine him urging Delia towards the gate.

'What about my earring?'

'I left it at the office. I'll drop it in to you on my way home tonight.'

Lifting her head up a little, Minta risked a look over the balcony. They were standing near the gate, their backs towards her and Dane had his hand on the other girl's arm. Delia turned to go, then she suddenly flung herself at him, her arms round his neck, her body against his in an attitude of familiar intimacy. 'Oh, darling, I can't stand being apart from you like this. Must we really wait so long before we can be together permanently again?'

Minta gasped with horror and slid down the balcony, her hands over her ears, unable to bear any more. Oh God, no! Please don't let this be happening to me. Don't let him do this to me. But when she opened her eyes the world was still there, real and suddenly terrible. The sound of Dane moving around downstairs reached her and then he called her name. Slowly she got to her feet. The sunglasses were still on the floor, where she had dropped them. They looked to be expensive. Minta lifted her sandalled foot and viciously smashed them to pieces. Walking out on to the landing, she moved to the head of the stairs and waited for Dane to come up to her.

He did so two at a time, his face lighting up when he saw her waiting for him. 'This is very convenient. Are you still ready for that siesta?' Reaching the top of the stairs, he put his arms round her waist and drew her towards him. 'I can hardly wait either.' There was nothing different in his manner, he would have seemed just the same if she hadn't known, if she hadn't been forced to hear.

'Is that what you want?' Minta asked woodenly.

'To take you to bed? Of course.'

'And do you want to make love to me?'

He looked amused. 'Most certainly. And I know just what I'm going to do to you. I've been thinking about it all morning.' As he spoke he had begun to undo the buttons at the front of her dress, pulling it aside to expose her breasts. He put up his hands, his fingers extended, to caress them, but as he did so Minta lifted her arm and struck him as hard as she could across the face, the ring she was wearing leaving a thin rake of torn flesh across his cheek.

'You liar!' she screamed at him as he staggered back, caught off balance and having to grab at the banister rail to stop himself from falling down the stairs. 'You bloody rotten liar. You cheat!' She came at him, arms flailing, fingers hooked like talons. 'I heard you—I heard you out there with her in the garden. Thinking about making love to me all morning? All you were doing was trying to phone *her*. Your mistress. That tramp!' Her voice filled with raging, incoherent sobs as she continued to lash out at him, tears pouring down her face.

'Stop it! Minta, stop it.' Dane tried to catch her arms, but she was filled with a mad kind of strength and he swore as she tore his shirt, her nails leaving trails across his chest. 'For God's sake listen to me. Minta! Oh, hell.' He gave her a push that sent her reeling backwards, then stepped quickly after her and caught hold of her wrists as she automatically tried to regain her balance.

'Darling, listen to me. I can explain . . .'

'Don't call me that! Don't call me that. I don't want your lousy explanations!' Pulling her head back, she jerked it suddenly forward, butting him in the face. He swore again so that she knew she'd hurt him and was fiercely glad. She struggled wildly, kicking out at his shins, but she was only wearing open-toed sandals and made little impact.

'For God's sake—you hellcat!' The words came out unevenly as Dane fought to keep hold of her. 'Be still!'

'You bastard! Let go of me!' Minta swore at him hysterically, completely oblivious of anything but the need to hurt him. She tried to kick him and he had to move quickly out of the way.

Suddenly angry himself, he said grimly, 'I've had enough of this.' Stepping forward, he caught hold of her arms and pinned them to her sides, holding her in a kind of bear-hug. For a moment he let her feel his strength and Minta realised that it was a man she was trying to fight, a man who was fit and hard and who could break her as easily as a fragile glass. But that didn't intimidate her; she went on yelling abuse at him, tears of frustrated anger in her eyes. And she struggled wildly, wriggling and kicking out at his shins, so that it took all his strength to hold her and carry her into the bedroom, where he dumped her unceremoniously on to the bed. Then he picked up the phone extension while Minta lay there, winded and trying to get her breath back.

When she moved to sit up, Dane pushed her back against the pillows. Quickly he finished speaking, put down the phone and sat on the edge of the bed, eyeing her warily.

But the fight had gone out of her and all Minta could

do was glare at him, her hazel eyes full of hate and despair. 'Who was that you were talking to—your mistress? I suppose you just couldn't wait to tell her.'

'No, it was the office. I told them I wouldn't be in this afternoon,' Dane answered levelly. 'We have to talk this out.'

'As far as I'm concerned there's nothing to talk about,' Minta said viciously. 'You can go to your mistress! I certainly don't want you around.'

'You know you don't mean that.' Dane tried to take hold of her hand but she pulled it away.

'Yes, I do. You can go to hell for all I care!' She turned away, unable even to look at him.

'Minta, listen to me.' He reached an arm across her so that she couldn't get away. His voice urgent, he said, 'All right, she was my mistress. But before I met you. Do you understand? I finished it the moment I got back here.'

'You liar,' Minta sobbed. 'She said she was just waiting to get back with you. Why the hell did you marry me if you didn't love me?'

'I *do* love you. I love you more than life itself. She must have known you were listening and said that just to try and mess things up between us. I told her there was no chance of my ever going back to her—didn't you hear me say that?'

Minta shook her head, remembering that she had covered her ears then.

Seeing her slight indecision, Dane immediately followed it up by saying, 'You asked the question yourself: why did I marry you and bring you here if I didn't love you?' He waited for her to answer, but when she didn't, just lay there with her head averted, he stood up. 'I'm thirty-two years old, Minta, and I have all the normal needs and appetites of a man. And Delia, to put it crudely, satisfied one of those appetites.'

'I don't want to know.' Minta shuddered and put her hands over her ears, but he immediately leaned over her and pulled them down again.

'Oh, no, you're going to listen to me whether you like it or not. You owe me that much.' He stared down at her for a moment, then took a breath and went on, 'Delia was over here working as a courier with one of the travel firms; she liked it and wanted to stay on during the winter. She'd heard about the time-share development and came to me looking for a job. I liked her and took her out and we ended up going to bed together.'

'And you gave her the diamond and ruby earrings just to say thank you for a one-night stand, I suppose?' Minta said jeeringly.

Dane flinched. 'No, because she was instrumental in helping me to buy a piece of land I needed. She'd heard that it might be for sale and contacted me so that I was able to make an offer and have it accepted before anyone else heard about it.'

'Payment for services rendered?'

'If you like, yes.'

'And what payment did you give her for the services she gave you in bed? *In this bed. In this house!*' Minta's voice rose, close to hysteria again.

'Easy!' He tried to take hold of her hand, but she wouldn't let him. 'When her job as a courier came to an end in September she didn't have anywhere to go. So I let her move in here.'

'With you?'

'Yes,' Dane answered, his voice quite steady. 'With me. It was—convenient, for both of us. And I couldn't know then that in a couple of months I would go to London and fall in love with you and marry you so quickly.'

He fell silent, watching her, then, after a long moment, Minta said reluctantly, 'Why did you bring me here—where you'd lived with her? And why did you lie?'

'Because everything had happened between us so quickly, and because of the row with your father. There was no time to come back alone and sort everything out before you joined me here. And okay, I didn't want you to find out. What man would in the circumstances? I got rid of Delia as soon as I could, and I brought you here because it's my home and because I knew you'd like it and be happy here. Delia seemed to understand and she promised to keep away, but I'm beginning to see now that leaving the earring here and pretending to come back for it was just a trick; she obviously intended to make trouble between us.'

Slowly Minta turned to look at him, there was a grim look to his mouth that boded no good for the other girl. 'She did,' she said slowly. 'She sent me up to the balcony for her sunglasses. She must have seen your car turn into the road.'

'I'm sorry.' This time his hand captured hers. 'I wouldn't have had this happen for the world.'

'Then you should have told me the truth in the first place. Before we left England,' Minta told him angrily.

'And wouldn't it have made any difference to the way you felt about me?'

'No, of course not! I . . .' Minta's voice broke off as she tried to imagine how she would have felt. Would she really have been so keen and willing to marry him if she'd known he had a live-in mistress?

'You see?' Dane said gently. 'It might have made you listen to your father. We might never have got married. I just *had* to take the risk of being able to sort it all out when I got home.'

Minta turned away and rolled off the bed, got to her feet. She stood looking at him for a moment and then down at the bed. 'You slept with her in that bed,' she accused.

'His jaw tightened. 'Yes.'

'I'm never going to sleep in it again.'

'Okay, so we'll get a new one, or sleep in the other bedroom.'

Minta glared at him. 'No, you can have it to yourself. Because I never want to share a bed with you again.' Dane's mouth hardened into a thin line, but before he could speak, she marched out of the room and down the stairs. He followed her to the hall and there she turned on him. 'Why don't you go to work? I'm tired and I want to rest.'

'I'm staying.'

'Oh, for God's sake! Can't you see that I want to be by myself? I don't want you near me.' Turning her head away, she put up a hand to cover her eyes, to hide the tears.

'Minta darling.' Dane came to put his hands on her shoulders but she shook him off.

'Just go away and leave me alone, can't you?' Her voice shook uncontrollably and she turned and ran out into the bright sunlight of the garden, through the trees to the small patch of grass, where she threw herself down and began to cry as if her heart would break.

Dane left her alone to cry herself out, but he didn't go back to the office, instead spreading plans and other papers out on the dining-room table and working there.

After a couple of hours he walked down the garden to find her.

Minta was still lying on the grass, but she had stopped crying and her eyes were closed. Dane thought she was asleep, but she wasn't; she knew full well that he was standing there, studying her, wondering whether or not to wake her. She kept her eyes closed, not yet ready to talk to him, and far from forgiving him, and after a few minutes he went back to the house. The sun was hot, she could feel it burning through her eyelids. Restlessly she turned her head and opened her eyes, looking towards the house. Everything had been so perfect, so idyllic; she had fallen in love with the house as she had fallen in love with Dane, both at first sight. And they could have been so happy here, if the past hadn't intruded so maliciously into the present.

It was hard to try to be objective about what had happened, but Minta could, to some extent, see Delia Nelson's point of view, because she knew how terrible she would feel herself if Dane came home and said she'd got to leave because he'd fallen in love with someone else. She, too, would want to lash out and hurt, but surely not in such a snide, deceitful way. Minta had been protected and sheltered all her life, cushioned from the blows that life could deal out, the only great sadness she had experienced being her mother's death, but now, within a short time, she had had to face losing her father's love and also finding out that Dane wasn't such a paragon as she had believed. She had known that he was experienced, of course, no man who was so wonderful in bed could be otherwise, and she realised that he had had to learn somewhere, but she hadn't really thought about him with other women, it was something she'd pushed to the back of her mind because she didn't want to think about him making love to anyone but herself. But now she had to face the fact that he had lived here in this lovely house with Delia, had lain naked with her in the big bed and done the wonderful things to Delia's body that he did to hers. Being a woman, Minta immediately wondered which of them he had preferred, whose body gave him the greatest pleasure, and she was filled with such a rage of jealousy that she turned and beat her fists against the ground, love for the moment turning to hate. How could Dane hurt her like this? How could he, when he said he loved her?

But it had been Delia Nelson who had deliberately set out to hurt her, purely out of spite, presumably, because even if Dane still had any feelings for her, her actions today would have completely alienated him. That she could have hoped to get him back this way was impossible. Minta tried to be fair, to see that it was the other woman's fault, but the mental pictures of the two of them together kept filling her mind and she couldn't forgive him. Not yet, it was too raw and hurtful.

When Dane came out to her again, she was sitting on the grass resting her chin on her knees. The sun had lost its warmth and there were long shadows across the garden.

'You'd better come in, it's getting chilly.'

'I'm not cold,' she returned, although her voice was arctic.

'Well, you must be hungry.'

'No.'

He crouched down beside her. 'I thought you were adult enough not to sulk, Minta.'

'I'm not—sulking.'

'Then come inside.' He straightened up and offered her his hand.

Minta looked up at him mutinously for a moment as she considered whether to defy him, but she hadn't liked being accused of sulking. Ignoring his hand, she got quickly to her feet and strode towards the house, head held high, letting him follow more slowly. He had prepared dinner; the table was laid and there was a salad with soup ready to heat on the cooker, and the crisp bread rolls she had bought that morning. Momentarily she was touched because she couldn't remember any man ever having prepared a meal with his own hands for her before, not even her father, but then she remembered the intimate meal that she had planned for them that night and her heart hardened. 'I told you—I'm not hungry,' she snapped.

Dane's face grew grim. 'You haven't eaten since breakfast.'

'I don't care. I don't want to eat here—where you sat with her.'

'All right,' he said patiently. 'We'll go out to eat.'

'No, I don't want to go anywhere with you. You can go and join your mistress for all I care. That's what you promised, isn't it? That you'd see her tonight to give her back her precious earring?'

'Minta, for heaven's sake.' There was exasperation in Dane's tone as he reached out for her.

'Leave me alone!' She pulled quickly away from him. 'I never want you to touch me again!' Then she turned and ran upstairs, locking herself into the spare bedroom at the back of the house.

She lay on the bed, half afraid, half hoping that he would come up after her and make her let him in. But he didn't come, and then she grew even more afraid that he would take her at her word and go to Delia Nelson. She lay on the bed, straining to hear the sound of the front gate, but it might be inaudible from here. For a long time there was complete silence and her heart grew gradually colder with fear, but then she heard the sound of the record player, and when she looked out of the window she saw a stream of light from the kitchen. She was hungry now, but pride prevented her from going down to get something to eat, instead she sneaked into the other bedroom for her nightdress, used the bathroom, then locked herself up again, lying awake for a long time, feeling extremely sorry for herself, especially when she heard Dane come up to bed, and she thought of what would have been happening if they'd been together. But he didn't even try the door handle to see if she'd locked him out.

Minta lay in the lonely bed, too restless and miserable to sleep. She knew that if she went to him everything would be all right again, that Dane would take her in his arms and kiss away all her doubts and fears. He had said when he came home at lunch time that he had worked out exactly what he wanted to do to her, and she couldn't help but wonder, with a thrill of erotic anticipation, what it was. But Delia Nelson's ghost lay like a physical presence between them. Would he already have done the same to his mistress? Would he be comparing the two of them, matching her own reaction against that of the other woman he had taken in that bed?

It was late when she woke the next morning and ventured downstairs. Dane had left, but he had written a note for her and left it propped up in the kitchen. 'I shall be at the office all day. If you telephone I'll come home immediately.' But she didn't phone, although she felt wretched all day, instead going for a long walk along the beach, barefoot, her feet splashing through the tiny waves breaking on the shore. During the afternoon a furniture van arrived from El Corte Inglés and parked outside the gate, almost completely blocking the road, much to the annoyance of some neighbours who wanted to get by. Minta and the delivery men had a bit of a language problem at first, but then they carried in a new double bed which they heaved upstairs, pulling the old one to pieces and taking it away with them. They also left a complete set of new bedding. After they had gone, Minta went up and looked at the bed, which they had put together, leaving the bedding still in its wrappers on top. If anything, she decided, the bed was even bigger than the old one. Dane certainly knew where his priorities lay—and his women, she thought with bitter irony.

She didn't attempt to make up the bed, but went downstairs again. Presumably she was supposed to be pleased that he was trying to conciliate her, but somehow it only made her angry. He needn't think all it would take to get her sweet again was a new bed!

When Dane came home that evening, Minta didn't even comment about the bed, she set a meal in front of him, told him that she'd already eaten and left him to go in the sitting-room and read a magazine. After he had finished his meal she heard him clearing up in the kitchen, then he came into the sitting-room and poured himself a drink, his grey eyes on her bent head. Crossing to an armchair, he sat down, casually stretching his long legs. After a long silence that seemed to go on for ever, he said, 'I see the new bed arrived safely.'

'Yes.' Minta didn't bother to raise her head.

'Do you approve of my choice?'

She shrugged indifferently. 'It's okay, I suppose.'

'Perhaps you'll give me a hand to make it up later?'

Closing the magazine, she tossed it on to the coffee table and stood up. 'Make it up yourself; you're the one who'll be sleeping in it.' Then she hurried from the room.

'Minta!' Dane's voice called after her, but she kept going to the spare room and didn't go down again that night.

The next evening was much the same; Dane ate alone and when he came into the sitting-room and started talking to her, Minta immediately got up to leave. But this time he was ready for her and caught her arm as she went by.

'Just how long do you intend to keep this up?' he demanded grimly. 'I already told you I have no time for sulky women.'

'Oh, really? I thought you had time for any women,' Minta shot back impulsively.

The grip on her arm tightened until it hurt, but she steeled herself not to let him see. 'Just don't try me too far,' he threatened. 'My patience is rapidly wearing thin!'

Minta glared back at him silently and he suddenly let her go and turned away, a dark, fed-up look on his face.

Being alone that night was self-inflicted torture. Minta's body was on fire with need of him. They had been together such a short time, but her body had become used to having him love her, it ached with longing to be touched, filled, pleasured. She wanted him so much. Her loins longed for his hardness as she turned restlessly on the pillow, unable to sleep, wondering if Dane, too, was lonely, if he wanted her as much as she wanted him. But perhaps he was thinking of Delia Nelson or some other girl he'd known before he met her. With a sob, Minta turned her face into the pillow, thinking that she'd go crazy with doubt and jealousy, and eventually cried herself to sleep.

The next day was Friday, and the weekend when they would be alone together loomed ahead of her like a threat, whereas last week she had looked forward to it with joyful anticipation. Dane came home earlier, before she had prepared the meal.

'We'll eat out,' he informed her, his jaw determined.

Minta started to protest that she'd got food in, then shrugged. 'All right, if that's what you want.'

They went up to their separate rooms to change and she deliberately kept him waiting, taking her time over her hair and make-up, changing her mind three times about what she would wear, and at last going down in a full silk skirt with matching sleeveless top and a little jacket. Dane was waiting for her in the garden, dressed in a dark suit that accentuated his height and slimness, a drink in his hand. He made no comment on her tardiness, but he didn't tell her how lovely she looked either, which he had always done before whenever they had gone out. And Minta found that she missed that—very much. Being proud wasn't any fun at all, she thought dismally as Dane silently led her out to the car.

They had dinner at a rooftop restaurant back in the tourist area of the town, sitting at a table looking out over the bay, which was outlined now by hundreds of lights strung along the shoreline like jewelled necklaces. Over on the far side of the room a small group played muted, tuneful melodies, and some of the customers got up to dance between courses. Dane didn't ask her to dance until they had finished their meal and were sitting over their liqueurs, then he quite deliberately put a hand over hers where she rested it on the table. 'Let's dance, shall we?'

'No.' Minta's reply was cold and abrupt, and she quickly drew her hand away.

Dane's hand balled into a fist and his face tightened into a set mask. In that instant Minta knew that his patience had snapped and he wouldn't take no for an answer again. A thrill of fear, all mixed up with a crazy kind of excitement, ran through her and she could hear her heart begin to beat loudly in her chest. Lifting a hand, he beckoned the waiter over and asked for the bill. When he had paid it, he stood up, his face still set in that cold mask. 'Let's go,' he commanded shortly.

He didn't say a word on the way home. Minta sat as far away from him as the confines of the car would allow and tried to work out how she could avoid a confrontation, but although he didn't speak, Dane's anger and determination filled the atmosphere, making the tension between them so strong that it was like an explosive charge, ready to detonate at any moment.

When they got to the house he had to get out to open the gates, drive the car in, then close the gates again. While he was doing the latter, Minta headed for the front door, her key ready in her hand, intending to run up to her room and lock herself in again, but Dane must have guessed what she was about, because he just swung the gates to and strode over to her.

'If you lock yourself in again, I'll smash the damn door down!' he threatened furiously.

Minta unlocked the door and turned defiantly. 'I shall sleep where I like. And if I want to lock my bedroom door I shall go ahead and do it!'

Before she had finished speaking, Dane lunged forward and grabbed her wrist, turning it so that she cried out and the door key fell to the ground. 'You're not going anywhere until we've had this out.' Still holding her wrist, he pulled her across the terrace into the garden.

'Let go of me! There's nothing to talk about.' Minta, too, was angry now, but it was anger that was all mixed up with intense excitement and exhilarated anticipation. She knew that there was only one way this would end and there was nothing she wanted more, but, perversely, she meant to make it as hard for him as she possibly could.

Dane reached the cleared, grassy area and pulled her round to face him, none too gently. There was a bright moon that shone its rays across his face, adding fire to the bright flame of anger in his eyes. 'I've had just about as much as I can stand of this!' he grated. 'For God's sake grow up and face facts. Did you really believe that I lived like a monk, just waiting and hoping for someone like you to come along?'

Minta stared into his face, shadowed by the moonlight, and thought that he looked more like a devil than a monk. She tried to pull her wrist free. 'I don't give a damn who you went with before you met me. Or what women you go with now, for that matter,' she added insultingly, knowing that it would inflame him.

It did. He dragged her roughly into his arms, his face white with anger. 'Don't you?' he demanded furiously. 'Don't you really care? How about if I brought Delia back here, then? Made love to her in the main bedroom while you slept alone in the back? Would you still not care?'

'Shut up! Shut up about her!' Minta yelled at him.

She struggled to get free, but he had her wrists firmly in his grasp.

'So that gets to you, does it? You don't like to think of me in bed with another woman, doing the things to her that I've done to you. Maybe you aren't as indifferent as you say you are. So let's find out, shall we?' With a quick movement, he took both her wrists in one hand behind her back, using the other to grab hold of her hair so that she couldn't move her head away without hurting herself. Then he bent her back against his braced body and lowered his head to kiss her.

Minta kept her mouth firmly closed, denying a response to his insinuating lips that touched, explored, caressed. His lips hardened then, became more demanding, but still she refused to submit. 'Open your mouth,' he commanded.

She glared at him out of hostile eyes. 'Go to hell!'

But she'd pushed him too far. With an oath, he let go her hair and his hand went to the thin straps of her top, jerking at them until the thin silk tore and the top slipped down to her waist.

'Stop it! How dare you tear my clothes! I . . .'

Her protests died away with a shuddering gasp as he found her breasts, handling them roughly, hurting her at first, but then becoming more gentle as he stroked and fondled her.

'Don't. Leave me alone!' A shudder of emotion, of need racked her, but still Minta tried to pull away. But then his fingers were followed by his mouth and she moaned in exquisite agony. Quickly then his lips were on hers again, hot and frenzied, assaulting her senses until at last she gave in to him, returning his kiss greedily. Dane let go her wrists so that he had both hands free to caress her. His mouth moved across the curve of her chin, the hollows of her cheeks. He caught the lobe of her ear between his teeth and bit gently, then his hot, sensuous lips moved down the column of her throat and found her breasts again.

Both of them were aroused to an intensity that made them tremble with desire. Minta curled her fingers in his thick hair and arched towards him, giving little groans of pleasure. Somehow they were lying on the grass and Dane tossed aside his jacket, lying on top of her, his weight pinning her down. They kissed hungrily, compulsively, rolling on the ground, while Minta's hands went to his shirt, the buttons tearing in her haste to undo them. The touch of his skin on hers was one of the most exquisite sensations she'd ever known. Dane cried out as she found herself on top of him and bent to suck and bite, rousing him to a frenzy. With a heave, he swung her off him on to the grass again, his eager hands pulling up her skirt. There was no time to take their clothes off, no time for anything but the savage, abandoned act of love, the assuagement of angry frustration in this passionate fusion of their bodies. They were completely lost in wild, ecstatic sexuality, until their bodies convulsed in mutual, searing pleasure.

CHAPTER SIX

THEY spent most of the weekend making love; in bed, in the garden, the bath, or any other part of the house they happened to be in when the need came upon them to re-establish and rediscover their former intimacy. And because of their disagreement, they loved with a deeper intensity, a stronger emotion. After that first time in the garden, Minta had clung to Dane, weeping tears of mingled joy and relief, begging him never to leave her, never to let her go.

'Oh God, I was so jealous,' she wept. 'I couldn't bear to think of you with anyone else. Swear that you don't love her. Please swear it!'

'I don't—I promise you, I don't.' Dane put his hands on either side of her head and kissed away her tears.

'But you had a love affair with her.'

'No, just an affair. I liked her, but love didn't come into it. It was understood that we were both free to end it whenever we wanted. But it was my fault; I should have realised that she felt vindictive.'

'No, it wasn't. It was her fault. But I suppose I can understand a little. I know how terrible I'd feel if someone took you away from me.'

'No one ever will,' Dane assured her thickly. 'I love you and only you. There'll never be anyone else.'

'Oh, darling, hold me—hold me tight. I don't ever want to be apart from you again.'

He held her trembling body close in his arms. It was very quiet, just the distant sound of the traffic on the main road and the faint music from someone's radio disturbing the peace of the night. The moonlight lay across them, turning their skin to silver. Minta put up a hand and lightly ran her fingers across Dane's bare chest, from silver to shadow.

'You remember that day you came home and found *her* here,' she began huskily.

'Don't talk about it,' he interrupted brusquely. 'It's over.'

'Yes, I know. But you remember you came home and said that you'd been thinking all morning about—about how you'd like to make love to me. Had you really been thinking about it?'

'Of course. And I remember exactly what I meant to do.'

'Tell me. It's been driving me crazy,' Minta admitted.

He laughed. 'No, I won't tell you.' He paused, watching the disappointment appear in her face. 'But I'll show you,' he said softly, with such a wealth of heady promise in his voice that she shivered in delighted anticipation.

Ignoring their discarded clothes, he picked her up and carried her inside and up to the bedroom.

In some ways those two days made up for the honeymoon they had never had. There were no inhibitions or shyness between them, nothing to stop them experiencing the exquisite pleasure of exploring each other's body, giving and taking pleasure with equal enjoyment. To Minta it seemed wonderful that she had the power to make him want her, and Dane hardly seemed to tire, was always hungry to sample the delights of her body. They seldom left each other's side for more than a few minutes, constantly needing the

reassurance of touch and nearness. There didn't seem to
be much point in wearing clothes either, for they were
constantly either taking them off or taking them off
each other. Once Minta went downstairs to prepare a
hot snack while Dane showered. She put on a bibbed
apron with a frill around it while she worked and still
had it on when she carried the meal into the dining-
room. Dane was already sitting down while she laid it
out, but then she turned round and he discovered that
she was completely naked beneath the apron, so the
meal was entirely forgotten as one bodily hunger was
replaced by another far more urgent one.

On the Monday Dane had to go to work again and
Minta arranged to meet him for lunch. He had a
slightly haggard look about the eyes from their long
weekend of love, but he walked tall, a new spring in his
step. After lunch he took her back to his office and
introduced her round. He didn't actually say so, but
Minta gathered that he hadn't taken her there before
because they had all known about Delia Nelson. He
had quite a large office suite on the second floor of a
new building in the commercial quarter of the town.
Most of the staff were Canarians except for one elderly
Englishman who had retired to the island and worked
part-time on the accounts. The walls of his personal
office were covered with maps and site plans of the
time-share development in different scales. Dane spent
quite some time explaining everything to her, showing
her photographs of the site before they had started and
describing how he intended to use the natural features
of the land, such as an outcrop of rock, making a pretty
waterfall, and incorporate them to enhance the aesthetic
appearance of the development.

'These are the plans of the villas,' he told her, taking

some papers from a folder. 'You see, they're basically two- or three-bedroomed and are fully self-catering, but we can also provide a four-bedroomed villa quite easily by knocking two of the two-bedroomed type into one. And we also have two blocks of studio apartments which are going to be built here on the side of the hill where there isn't enough space for any villas. That way we hope to get young couples coming here as well as families with children. What do you think of the designs?'

'They look great. Are the kitchens well equipped?'

Dane grinned. 'Trust a Cordon Bleu cook to ask that question! I haven't really gone into the details of the equipment for the kitchens yet. Or the decoration and furniture for the other rooms either, come to that.' He looked at her, his eyebrows rising in the slightly mocking way that she loved. 'How would you like to have a go at that job?'

Minta stared. 'Do you really mean it? But I know nothing about decorating, especially on a scale as large as this.'

'Your father told me that you'd chosen the décor for your house in London.'

'Well, yes, but . . .'

'Well, that looked pretty good to me. Why don't you take it one room at a time for one villa? I've got quotes for furniture and electrical equipment from a host of companies, but I need someone to choose and then marry everything up so that the villas look good. And it's important that we have the show villas ready as soon as possible so that people can come over and see them and buy their time-share ready for next summer.'

'Will the villas be ready for sale that soon?'

'They've got to be,' Dane replied grimly. 'That's why

it's so important that as much work as possible is put into this project now, during the off season. Tell you what,' he said less seriously, 'why don't you drive down to the site with me tomorrow and have a look round? Maybe you'll get some ideas.'

'Okay,' Minta agreed happily. 'And if you like I'll take all the leaflets and things you've got on furniture home with me now and study them. Then tomorrow I'll already have an idea what's available.'

'Marvellous!' Dane kissed her and she responded enthusiastically. 'Sex-cat,' he murmured against her mouth, his hands on her breasts. 'I've a good mind to lay you across my desk and take you.'

Minta giggled, loving every minute of it. 'Your staff would get a shock if someone came in and found us!'

'Mmm,' Dane agreed regretfully. 'Which is why we'll have to abandon the idea, I'm afraid.'

'Abandon?' she objected pertly. 'Why not just postpone it—until some time when there's no one else around? Then every time you sit at your desk afterwards you'll be able to remember the other use you made of it.'

'God,' Dane groaned, 'if I did that I'd never get any work done. You're a big enough distraction already. My mind keeps going to you when I should be working. And during those last few days, when you wouldn't let me near you . . .' He gave a rueful laugh. 'Lord, I must have been hell to work with! Don't ever do that to me again, Minta. I couldn't stand it.'

'Oh, I won't—I promise I won't. I missed you so much, and I wanted you so much. All of you. Loving me.'

'Idiot,' Dane said thickly. 'Come here.' Drawing her to him, he began to kiss her, his hands on her waist, then low on her hips, pressing her against him.

There was a sharp rap on the door and it was immediately opened, giving them no time to move apart. 'Oh, sorry.' It was the English accountant, who gave them a broad grin, in no way embarrassed. 'It's that roof tile company on the line; they insist on speaking to you personally.'

'Okay, I'll be right there. Send someone to get a taxi for my wife, will you?' The man went out, shutting the door behind him. Dane gathered up the folder of leaflets and a copy of each of the villa plans. 'You sure you don't mind having a go at this?'

'No, of course not. I shall enjoy it.' Putting her hands on his shoulders, Minta gazed into his face, almost as if she were committing each feature to memory: his unlined forehead, slightly arched brows, straight nose and strong chin, his mouth which gave a hint of his high sexuality in the lower lip, and his eyes, long-lashed and clear grey, that looked back at her with such emotion in their depths that she suddenly felt too choked up to speak and could only cling to him, blinking back tears.

'I know,' he said softly, his mouth close to her ear. 'I know.'

Then he let her go and they smiled at each other, the unspoken vow of love between them, the promise of its fulfilment implicit in their eyes.

For Minta the next few weeks were the happiest in her life. Most times that Dane had to visit the holiday development site she went with him, taking samples of material and paint charts with her, measuring, working out sizes and colour schemes. And often in the evenings they would sit together, the plans spread out on the dining-room table as soon as the meal was cleared away, discussing her ideas, Dane pointing out any impracticalities, but mostly falling in with her and pleased that she was taking such an interest.

'I'm putting you on our pay-roll,' he told her. 'You'll get your first salary cheque at the end of the month.'

'But I don't want any money,' Minta objected. 'I'm enjoying it.'

'Even so, you're doing a job and you should be paid for it. If I got a firm who specialise in that kind of thing to do it they'd expect to be paid, now wouldn't they?' Bending forward, he kissed the tip of her nose.

'I suppose so. What's so fascinating about the end of my nose?'

'I find every part of you fascinating and would like to kiss them all.'

Minta flushed and said huskily, 'I think you already have. At least, I can't think of any bits that you've missed.'

'In that case I shall have to start all over again, won't I?' And he lifted his hand to begin undoing her blouse, their work forgotten.

During the day, when Dane was at his office, Minta spent long, but contented hours scouring the island for the things she needed to furnish the villas, gradually getting to know the island and overcoming the language problem with the help of a middle-aged Canarian, José, who spoke English and who had been hired specially to drive the car that Dane had obtained for her use. It gave her a great thrill whenever she tracked down a manufacturer who was willing to supply them direct, and she often got a good bargain, thanks mainly to José, who was a born haggler and who was willing to go on bargaining long after Minta would have given up.

But her greatest delight, as the days passed, was the

growing certainty that she was pregnant. Each day she woke, afraid that she might be wrong, then gave a sigh of pleasure when there was still no sign. She hugged the knowledge to her, wanting to be absolutely certain before she said anything to Dane, her silence in some way acting as an insurance policy against anything going wrong. Although he must guess, of course. By now he knew her body as well as she did, better perhaps. But he, too, didn't say anything, content to leave it to her. Minta decided that she would tell him at Christmas. She would give him the most wonderful Christmas present it was in a woman's power to bestow. And perhaps in her growing awareness of maternity, in some new-found maturity, or perhaps just because it was Christmas, Minta decided that after she had told Dane she would also write to her father and tell him the news, try to make it up with him. After all, he was her only relation and he had a right to know that he was to be a grandfather.

It seemed strange, as the December days went by, to go Christmas shopping in a summer dress with the sun shining and the trees full of leaves. The town, if anything, was busier, full of pale-skinned tourists escaping from the European winter, especially retired people who spent the whole season in the warmer climate, without fear of bronchitis and rheumatism, and all the other ills that dog the old during the harsh winter months. Minta had to make do with an artificial tree of silver tinsel which at first seemed a poor substitute for the large evergreen that had every year filled the house with the bittersweet scent of pine back in London. But she bought ornaments and a set of lights and spent hours making decorations until the living-room, once the curtains were closed, was as festive as any in Britain, although she would have liked an open fire to add the finishing touch to the room.

Their relationship now was almost as perfect as any two people could attain. Minta lived for Dane in that she missed him whenever he was away and looked forward eagerly to his return. Her thoughts were always full of him, of how she could please him in even the smallest ways: cooking meals that he liked, keeping the house welcoming, making herself look as attractive for him as she could. And always ensuring that she kept him happy in bed. They had never spoken of Delia Nelson again after they had made up, but it was always there at the back of Minta's mind, and she wanted to be sure that Dane never thought of the other girl with even a shadow of regret.

With the help of José she was beginning to learn Spanish, although Dane teased her that she would have a Canarian accent, and she was learning the correct amounts of food to buy in metric weights and how to ask for them in the market. Sometimes, too, she would persuade José to let her take over the car on the country roads so that she was gradually getting used to driving on the right and the crazy way that some of the islanders drove. And she cooked dinner nearly every night now, the two of them content to stay at home, although Dane would sometimes phone and impulsively tell her to change and insist they go out, taking her dining and dancing till the early hours of the morning. Whatever he wanted to do she was happy, so long as she was with him, able to reach out and touch him, hear his voice, have the reassurance of his nearness.

What to buy him for Christmas was a pleasant problem; Minta had bought him lots of small things but couldn't decide on his main present, torn between half a dozen ideas, but then she found a really beautiful modern leather documents case in El Corte Inglés which she was sure he would appreciate. She took it home in triumph, wrapping it immediately so that he wouldn't see it, hiding it for good measure, in the back of the deep, old-fashioned wardrobe in the spare bedroom. As she pushed the jumble of shoe boxes and bags aside to find a space for the parcel, Minta saw the brightness of material and pulled it out, thinking that one of her dresses must have fallen off a hanger. But then she recognised the dress as the one she had been wearing on the disastrous day that Delia Nelson had played that cruel trick on her—on them both. Minta remembered now that she had taken the dress off and in a fit of temper thrown it into the wardrobe, too angry to hang it up. Holding it up to the light, she saw that the dress was terribly creased and there were grass stains on it where she had lain in the garden and cried. It would have to be washed. As she carried the dress over to the laundry basket, she automatically put her hand into the pockets to check that they were empty, but she came to a standstill as she took out a piece of paper and recognised it as the one Delia Nelson had given her with her address on it.

For a long moment Minta stood perfectly still in the middle of the room, remembering, but then she gave an impatient exclamation. It was all over; Delia Nelson was no danger to her now. She had Dane and she had the child growing inside her. She began to crumple the paper into a ball, but then something made her stop and slowly straighten it out. The address was there, but there was a lot more writing besides, far too much for the other girl to have written at the time. She must have prepared this beforehand, as she had carefully planned the whole thing. It read: 'Today you will find out the truth about Dane and me. He doesn't love you. He married you only for your father's money. If you don't believe me, ask him where he got the backing for his time-share project. He intends to make you pregnant as soon as possible so that he'll have a greater hold on your father through the child. As for you, once the child is born you'll be dispensable, and he'll be able to come back to me permanently—the woman he really loves.'

Minta's first reaction was to tear the paper into shreds, to burn it. Anything to take the foul words out of her mind, to wipe them out as if they'd never been. But they were there, burning into her brain. After a few minutes she tried to look at it rationally, to see it as the cruel barbs of a jealous woman, making trouble in the only way she could, but two things got to her every time. First, that Dane had indeed made her pregnant as soon as he could, and secondly that he had never told her exactly from whom he had got the financial backing for his business. Back in London, Dane had told her that he had had several contacts and she had taken it for granted that one of those had agreed to back him after her father had refused, although, now she came to think of it, he had been pessimistic about it until the day after their wedding when he had had to leave her to go to a meeting. And then everything had been okay. But she had been far too preoccupied with her own concerns and emotions to question him about it very closely. Her whole life had changed over those two days and she had had little time for anything outside her personal feelings.

Now she began to wonder and worry. She sat on the edge of the bed, staring at the piece of paper, almost willing it to answer all the questions it had raised. It said that once her child was born she would be dispensable. What the hell did that mean? It couldn't possibly mean that Dane would want to be rid of her? Surely not even Delia Nelson, her mind twisted by jealousy, could think that? Even if he tried to divorce her he wouldn't be able to keep the child, no court in the world would allow it. The only way he could keep her child without her would be if she was mad or dead or something. Minta froze suddenly, all the gangster films she had ever watched on television where that phrase had been used flooding into her mind.

'Oh, God!' She got to her feet and began to pace the floor, furious that her happiness was again threatened, and from the same source. She'd like to kill Delia Nelson. Kill her, kill her, kill her! Which was probably exactly what the other girl must have felt about her when Dane brought her back here. The thought dispersed some of her anger and she went downstairs, automatically beginning to cook the evening meal. It was crazy of her to even begin to suspect Dane. It was just another attempt to break them up. And she had to remember that the note was written weeks ago. If Delia Nelson had been serious in her accusations why hadn't she followed them up, sent her another letter or something? Anyone could guess that she might become pregnant quite soon, there was nothing to stop them, after all. So the only real question was about the financial backing, and she could ask Dane about that tonight. As for him not loving her—he'd said so and shown her how much a thousand times; didn't that count for more than the ravings of a jealous woman?

Nonetheless, Minta picked her moment carefully

before she asked the all important question that evening. She waited until they had finished eating and were sitting at the table drinking coffee. 'Did you go over to the site today?' she asked.

'No, there was no need. I was interviewing some nurserymen who'd quoted for planting trees and shrubs once the first phase of building is done.' He gave a slight frown. 'I thought I'd already told you that.'

'Did you?' She gave a little nervous laugh. 'I must have forgotten. Everything seems to be going well, then?'

'Yes, fine. Better than I could have hoped. Thanks in a large part to you,' he smiled at her.

'And yet you were so worried that you wouldn't get the backing that you needed when you were in London. Who did you get it from in the end?' she asked, trying to sound casual, but her eyes fixed intently on his face.

Dane had been about to lift his coffee cup to his lips, but his hand stilled in mid-air and his face took on a set look. Minta felt her heart go cold. 'That's rather a funny question to ask now, isn't it?' he said lightly, drinking from the cup.

'Is it? I just wondered who we're indebted to, that's all.'

'Indebted is hardly the word. I haven't had to actually borrow any money from them yet. And I won't have to at all if we manage to sell the first units.'

'But you could if you wanted to?' Minta interrupted as he was about to go on.

'Yes, if it was absolutely necessary. But we've started advertising through agents in Britain and, as you know, the first people will be coming out to see the site and the show villa immediately after Christmas. Once they sign up the word will spread and we'll be away.'

'That's great,' Minta agreed. 'But I can see that you wouldn't have been able to go ahead unless you'd had substantial financial backing behind you. So who did back you?' she asked for the second time, her heart in her mouth.

Dane got up and moved over to the drinks cabinet, his back to her. 'Would you like a liqueur?'

'No, thanks.' She waited, her hands clenched together under the table. Surely he wouldn't try to change the subject again?

He poured himself a brandy and stood looking broodingly down as he swirled the liquid in the glass. At last he said, 'It was a consortium. No one company was willing to take on the whole thing, but they were each willing to take a part.'

'I see. Some of Daddy's friends were probably involved, then. Perhaps I know some of them.'

'Possibly. But I wasn't given all the names myself. They simply came under a group heading.' He turned and looked at her, his eyes watchful, a note of suspicion in his voice. 'You seem very interested in the subject suddenly.'

'Do I?' Minta tried her best to sound offhand. 'It must be because I was reading an article in the financial pages of the paper.'

Dane smiled, and to her eyes there was a trace of relief in it. 'Let me do the worrying about money—not that there's anything to worry about—and you concentrate on decorating the villas. The show house is almost ready for the furniture now.'

'Good.' But she didn't pick up his change of subject. 'I want to share everything with you, Dane. Everything,' she pleaded, getting to her feet.

'Of course. And I you.' His eyes travelled down her,

seemed to come to rest on her stomach, eloquently suggesting that she wasn't sharing everything with him.

Minta almost told him then, but something made her hold back. Now wasn't the time, not in these circumstances. Deliberately she talked of other things and the subject wasn't mentioned again. But that night, when they went to bed, Dane's lovemaking seemed to have a fierce determination about it, almost as if, if she wasn't pregnant already, then he was quite sure that he was going to make her so tonight. When it was over and he had fallen asleep, Minta lay awake beside him, her body aching and her mind in turmoil. He'd actually told her nothing, and his prevaricating had only served to increase her doubts.

During the night she realised that there was one way she could check on whether or not it was her father's bank that had backed Dane without either Dane or her father knowing. Richard Tennant employed a personal secretary who had worked for him at the bank for years and whom Minta had known all her life. If she phoned the secretary she was sure that she could persuade him to tell her all that she wanted to know. But even though she knew it would set her mind at rest, she didn't make the call all the next day or the day after, although her eyes often went to the phone, resting on it for minutes together as she worried about what to do. Perhaps subconsciously she was giving Dane the chance to tell her himself, to reassure her and put an end to all her doubts. She tried to act naturally when he was around, but he obviously noticed something, because on the second evening he asked her whether anything was the matter.

'What makes you ask that?' Minta prevaricated, trying to give herself time to think.

It was late in the evening and they were in their bedroom, preparing for bed. She had on a blue shortie nightshirt which buttoned all the way down the front, and was sitting at the dressing-table brushing her hair.

Dane came over and put his hands on her shoulders, looking at her in the mirror. He was wearing just the bottom half of his pyjamas, his chest bare. Minta couldn't help seeing the reflection of his broad shoulders, the muscles in his arms and the strength of his body. Just looking at him woke desire in her, and the touch of his hands, gently massaging her shoulders, sent it coursing through her body in waves, filling her with the familiar, aching need for him.

'I think I know you well enough by now to know when something's troubling you,' he told her.

'It's nothing. I'm fine, really.' His hands grew still and she said on a note of pleading, 'Go on. Don't stop.'

He began again, his hands strong but gentle, and Minta closed her eyes, wanting to forget everything else. Presently his hands moved down to the buttons on the front of her nightshirt, undid them and parted the material. 'Open your eyes,' he commanded softly.

Slowly she obeyed him and saw herself in the mirror, her breasts uncovered, the nipples hardened with desire.

'Is this what you want?'

She watched his hands begin to caress and explore, toying, squeezing, his fingers tanned against her white skin. It was the most erotically sensual experience Minta had ever known, and her body took fire as she gave little gasping moans of pleasure.

'Is this what you want?' he insisted.

'Yes. Oh, yes!' Minta breathed on a deep sigh.

'Tell me what's the matter. Tell me,' Dane commanded, his fingers hurting her now.

Opening her eyes, she saw that he was staring at her reflection, a tough, determined set to his jaw. Quickly she put up her hands and covered his, holding them still. She wanted to tell him the truth, but there was such a harsh look in his face. He didn't seem like Dane, like the man she loved. This was some stranger, someone she didn't recognise. Suddenly frightened, she blurted out, 'I—I think I'm going to have a baby.'

His eyes stared into hers in the mirror for a moment, then he pulled her to her feet and spun her round to face him. 'Darling! Oh, darling, that's wonderful news!' Lifting her up in his arms, he swung her round, laughing up at her. 'And there was I thinking all sorts of terrible things! But this—this is wonderful. We must celebrate.'

Minta laughed down at him, all her doubts overwhelmed by his exuberance. 'What? Right now?'

'Of course right now. What better time is there?' He sat her gently on the bed. 'Wait right there. I'll only be a minute.'

And he was as good as his word, running down the stairs and returning almost immediately with a bottle of champagne and two glasses.

'Champagne! I didn't know we had that.'

'I've been keeping it hidden away against just this moment.' He undid the metal cap and the cork came off with a bang, the golden liquid frothing over, but Dane skilfully caught it and filled the two glasses. 'Here.' He raised his glass, his eyes warm. 'To our child—and his beautiful mother.'

Minta clutched the glass in both hands, that ghastly letter intruding even now into what should have been one of the most wonderful moments in her life. 'You're sure you don't mind?'

'My darling girl! Do I look as if I mind? I couldn't be more pleased.'

'You don't think it's too soon?'

'No, I don't. Drink,' he said softly, pushing the glass towards her mouth.

Minta did so almost reluctantly, the demon in her mind unable to dismiss the fact that his reaction would be exactly the same whether the letter was true or false.

After they had drunk the toast he put an arm round her and they leant back against the headboard. 'Are you feeling all right—not sick or ill?'

'No, but it's early days yet. I wanted to be completely sure before I told you, but you insisted.'

'I don't like to see you troubled. And you did say that you wanted to share everything—remember?'

'Yes, I know.' She stared into his face, trying to find the truth, desperately wanting to convince herself that his reaction was genuine. Should she tell him about the letter? But if she did he would only laugh at her fears, tell her that it was all stupid lies. And that was what she wanted, so why didn't she just come right ought and tell him?

'When?' he was asking. 'When will it be born?' His hand went to the soft curve of her stomach, almost as if he was searching for the life growing there.

'I'm not sure. July or August, I suppose. I haven't been to a doctor yet.'

'Then you must—at once.' He was immediately all concern. 'I'll make an appointment for you to see the best doctor on the island tomorrow.' He hesitated, then added, 'And as soon as you're absolutely sure, I think we ought to let your father know.'

Yes. Yes, that's what you'd want, to be sure of my father's money, Minta thought, turning her head away.

But Dane misinterpreted her silence. Gently he said, 'I know you're still angry with him, darling, but he has a right to know about the baby.'

'Maybe I'll tell him when it's born,' she answered after a moment. 'Can I have some more champagne?'

'Of course.' He refilled her glass and kissed her. 'The only real place to drink champagne is in bed.' Her nightshirt was still open and he bent to kiss her breasts. 'I think I'm going to be a little jealous of this baby, when it arrives. And you must take care of yourself. We don't want any accidents. Promise me you'll be careful.'

'Yes, all right.'

He kissed her again and smoothed the hair back from her forehead. 'You'd better get some sleep. You're going to need all your strength from now on.'

Rather shakily, Minta asked, 'Aren't we going to finish the champagne?'

'Oh, no. Too much alcohol is bad for babies, that I do know.' Taking the glass from her, he set it down on the bedside cabinet and reached to turn off the light, but she stopped him.

Almost hating herself for doing so, but quite unable to ignore the aching need in her body, Minta said huskily, 'Dane?'

He hesitated. 'I don't want to hurt the baby.'

'You won't.' She hastened to reassure him, her voice betraying her urgency. 'It's quite safe—honestly.'

'You're sure? Well, if that's the case ...' His hands unbuttoned her nightshirt all the way down. 'I'll go back to where I left off.'

Their lovemaking that night was almost perfect. Dane had never been so tender and gentle with her. But it didn't help; the doubts were still there, driving her crazy, and Minta knew that she just had to find out the

truth. The next morning she waited until Dane had left
and then put a call through to London. She had to wait
over two hours for the call to be connected and had to
pretend that it was a personal call for her father's
secretary so that no one at the bank would recognise
her name. She spoke to him for some time, persuading
him to tell her what she wanted to know, and
afterwards making him promise to say nothing of her
call to her father. And because she'd always been able
to twist him round her little finger, he reluctantly
agreed.

When she replaced the receiver, Minta sat for a long
time, gazing blindly into space, all her worst fears
confirmed. The secretary had told her that it had in fact
been her father who had sent for Dane the day after
their wedding and given him the backing he needed,
telling the secretary privately that he had no other
choice; he couldn't let his daughter be married to a man
who was liable to go bankrupt within months. And
she'd learnt something else, too; the real reason why her
father hadn't wanted to risk the bank's money on Dane.
It seemed that his brother had inherited a big estate and
a great deal of money, but had just thrown it away on
gambling and ill-advised business ventures. That was
bad enough, but could be put down to stupidity, but
then he had gone to several merchant bankers,
borrowing money from them to finance another, but
non-existent business deal this time, and fraudulently
used the names of several well-known people, claiming
that they were in the venture with him. Of course it all
came out eventually, but by then Dane's brother had
gambled away all the money in one last desperate
attempt to recoup all his losses, and there was nothing
left. When the fraud was discovered, he tried—as

unsuccessfully as he did everything else, apparently—to kill himself. What was left of the family estate in Warwickshire had to be sold to help pay off the debts, but no prosecution had been brought against him because he had suffered a severe nervous breakdown after the suicide attempt and he was now permanently in a nursing home. So it was little wonder that neither her father's bank nor any other would finance Dane when he came looking for backing.

Minta got up and began to pace up and down the room, her arms folded across her chest in a protective attitude. Dane must have known how little chance he stood when he went to London, so why go there? Unless he had tried everywhere else first and was absolutely desperate. Desperate enough even to marry a girl he didn't love so that he could coerce her father into giving him what he wanted? Oh, God! No wonder Daddy hadn't wanted her to marry him. He could have told her about Dane's brother, but he hadn't; either because he had been told in confidence or because he didn't think she'd listen to him anyway. And she wouldn't have done, not then, not when she was so besotted by Dane. She knew that she would only have insisted that what had happened to Dane's brother had nothing to do with Dane. Why, they weren't even full brothers, only half-brothers.

And she was still besotted by him. But now things were different. Now she knew that he had lied to her twice: about his financial backing and about Delia Nelson. And most of the things in that rotten letter seemed to be coming true. Minta went to the window and leaned her head against the pane. There was no sun today, the skies were overcast and grey, as wretched as her feelings. If she wasn't so crazy about him it would be easy, she could just face him with it and if she wasn't satisfied with his answers, walk out and leave him. But she still loved him, more now than ever, and the thought of even distrusting him, let alone leaving him, was completely unbearable.

A wave of nausea filled her chest and throat and she had to sit down and take deep breaths, her child for the first time making its presence felt. Almost as if to remind her that she had that, too, to worry about. That her responsibilities were no longer only to herself.

She had wept before when she had found out about Delia Nelson, but this time she was too miserable even to cry. Her mind and heart were tortured by uncertainty. There could be some explanation for Dane's not telling her about her father's backing, just as he had had an explanation for not telling her about Delia Nelson. And she'd accepted that, hadn't she? So why not give him a chance, listen to him again? Going upstairs to the drawer where she had hidden the letter, Minta took it out and read it through again, although she knew its contents almost off by heart now. The one phrase that would prevent her ever facing Dane with the letter leapt out at her: 'Once the child is born you'll be dispensable.' Would that, too, come to be the truth as the other accusations had? She shivered convulsively and groaned aloud. 'No, oh, please, no!' Her heart wrestled with her mind in an anguish of uncertainty, but then she could stand it no longer; picking up her bag, she hurried out into the street and took a taxi to the address on the letter.

Delia Nelson's flat was in a new block built on one of the steep hillsides on the outskirts of the town because there was no flat land left to build on. Minta took the lift to the fourth floor and pressed the bell, hoping that

the other girl would be at home. She was. She opened
the door wearing a short-sleeved sweater and a straight
skirt, as slim and sophisticated as ever. Her eyes
widened a little when she saw Minta, but she merely
said, 'I wondered when you'd show up,' and held the
door open for her to go in.

'What made you so sure I'd come?' Minta countered,
as soon as the door was closed behind them.

'You were sure to find out the truth about Dane's
backer some time. And I figured that then you'd want to
know the rest.' Delia had led the way into a small but
compact kitchen where the ingredients for a salad were
spread out on the worktop. 'I'm just making myself
some lunch. Do you want some?'

'No.' Minta sat down at the small table, not trusting
her legs to hold her.

'Morning sickness?' the other girl asked, looking at
her shrewdly.

Minta stared. 'How did you know?'

'Dane told me, of course. You didn't really think
he'd stopped seeing me, did you?'

'Yes,' Minta answered slowly. 'He told me he'd never
see you again.'

'And you believed him? But then he could make any
girl believe anything he wanted her to. I know, he tried
it on me, too,' said Delia, her voice sounding bitter.

'What do you mean?'

Delia looked at her contemplatively for a moment,
then shrugged and came to sit opposite her. 'I suppose I
might as well tell you. Perhaps it'll help you to
understand. Did you know that Dane needed a certain
piece of land before he could go ahead with his time-
share village?' Minta nodded. 'Well, he probably didn't
tell you that I helped him to get it.'

'Yes, he did. He said that you found out that it was being sold and told him so that he could get in and buy it first. He said that was why he was grateful to you and gave you the earrings.'

'My God, is that what he said?' The other girl laughed loudly. 'I told you he could make people believe anything he wanted them to! The truth is that he used me to find out about that land. The owner fancied me and Dane persuaded me that if I really loved him I'd go to bed with the owner, the price being letting Dane have first refusal of the land.' Seeing the look of horror on Minta's face, she said angrily, 'There's no need to look at me like that. I love him! More than you do, because you'd never give yourself to someone else for his sake. Do you think I enjoyed what I did? Do you think it doesn't make me sick every time I think about it?'

Minta turned away, her hands gripping each other on the table. 'I'm sorry. It's just so difficult ...' She was silent as she gathered her courage to ask the last, all-important question. 'In your letter, you said that after my baby was born I'd be dispensable. What—what did you mean?'

Delia Nelson stared at her for a long moment, then got to her feet and turned away. 'Maybe I shouldn't have written that; I don't know. But I wanted to warn you. I only suspect ... It isn't your fault you got caught up in this.' She swung round. 'Look, all I mean is— well, after the kid's born, I wouldn't advise you to go swimming with Dane. You're not a good swimmer, and people drown in these seas. And don't go walking in heavy traffic with him; there are lots of accidents to pedestrians in Las Palmas. And never ...'

'Stop it! Stop it, do you hear me?' Minta was on her

feet and shouting at the other girl. 'It isn't true, any of it. You're just making it up. You just want him for yourself!'

'Yes, of course I want him!' Delia yelled back. 'What woman wouldn't? But not that way. I don't want any harm to come to you; that's why I tried to warn you. I hoped you might even leave him when you found out about us, but I guessed he'd talk you round, that's why I left the note.'

'I don't believe it. I can't believe it,' Minta moaned, her head in her hands.

'Of course you do. Look at yourself in the mirror. Why on earth do you think he married you when he had me? What attraction had you for him other than your father's money?'

'That isn't true. He loves me. We make love all the time,' Minta retorted desperately.

'Oh, sure. Dane's a very highly sexed man. For the time being he can't have me every day, so you'll do; and anyway, he had a reason to—he wanted to make you pregnant to make sure of you in case your father told you that he'd backed him and you began to suspect the truth. And your father would hardly abandon his only grandchild, even if you weren't around any longer, now would he? But he comes here often and we make love. How else do you think I know all about you? He laughs about you; about the way you threw yourself at him in London. About your clumsiness in bed, the way he has to show you everything.'

'Shut up! Shut up!' Her face chalk white, Minta stared at her tormentor, the cruel words beating into her brain. Delia's outline began to blur and swim in front of her eyes. Putting out an unsteady hand, she encountered the back of a chair and gripped it hard, trying desperately to fight off waves of blackness.

'Are you all right?' asked Delia, her voice sharp.

Minta didn't answer but plunged towards the door, groping blindly for the handle and reeling down the hallway as if she was drunk, her hand against the wall to steady herself.

'Wait! Where are you going? You can't leave in that state!'

But Minta didn't even hear her. Somehow she got out of the flat and into the lift, sagging against the wall as it took her down to the ground floor. She began to walk along the street, bumping into people and things like a blind person. Once she tripped over a broken paving stone and fell headlong, grazing her knees and hurting her arm. Someone helped her to her feet and said something to her in Spanish, but she only muttered a thank-you and went unsteadily on. Eventually she came to a square with lots of tables outside a *bodega*. The tables were empty today, the weather too chilly to tempt the tourists to sit outside. Gratefully Minta collapsed into a chair; she felt sick and ill and someone seemed to be stabbing a knife repeatedly into her head. She had been sitting there for some time before a waiter noticed her and grudgingly left the warmth of the bar to ask her what she wanted.

'Brandy. A large brandy,' she managed, then, seeing he didn't understand, 'Cognac. *Granda*,' demonstrating with her hands.

When it came, she drank half of it at a gulp, choking a little as the fiery spirit went down. But it did her good. The world came back into focus again and she didn't feel so sick any more. At least, not physically. Mentally she just wanted to die. Even now, with so much evidence against him, she still couldn't entirely believe that Dane had deceived her. Surely no man could appear to be so loving and not mean it? Her hand shook on her glass, as she remembered their lovemaking. But then she recalled that last night it had been she and not Dane who had wanted to; he had been willing to just turn off the light and go to sleep. Because now that he'd made her pregnant he didn't have to make love to her any more? The thought came into her mind like death into life.

Minta swallowed down the rest of the brandy and wondered what on earth she was going to do. More than anything else in the world she wanted to pretend that everything was the same, to just forget all the doubts and fears and go on as they had before. Because she loved and needed Dane so much. No matter what he'd done she would never be able to stop loving him. As well to ask the trees not to flower or the birds not to sing. Meeting Dane and falling in love with him was the most wonderful thing that had happened in her life, and nothing could change that. Not even the fact that he'd been lying to her all along. But loving him, knowing the truth, and going on living with him, were two different things. For the baby's sake, if not for her own, she couldn't go on living a lie. And as for him wanting to get rid of her—she would never believe that of him. He would have to hate her to want to do that. Surely he couldn't hate her—not after all the love they had shared. But if he could make Delia Nelson prostitute herself for him . . .

The chill thought filled her mind so that she was again unsure and afraid. She rested her elbow on the table and her head on her hand, praying silently for guidance, for all this worry and fear to be taken away from her. It was too much, she couldn't cope with it. Not now. Not when there was the baby too. She needed someone to take care of her, to take all the responsibility off her shoulders and make everything all right again.

That thought took her mind immediately to her father. All her life he had protected her and helped her make all the big decisions she had had to face. The only time she hadn't listened to him had been over Dane. And because of that he had washed his hands of her, wanted nothing more to do with her. Since her marriage he had made no attempt to get in touch with her, although he could quite easily have found out her address from one of her friends, or written to her care of Dane's company address. So going to him for help was out. Minta had too much of her father's own stubborn pride to go running back to him cap in hand, and there was also the fact that by going back home she would admit that Richard Tennant had been right and Dane didn't really love her. And she couldn't admit that even to herself.

So she was on her own. For the first time in her life she would have to cope by herself, with no one to help her. And what she decided could alter the whole course of her life. Minta sat on at the table for a long time, gradually getting more and more chilled but unable to find the strength to get up and walk away. After an hour or so the waiter came out again and she ordered a coffee, but she hadn't finished drinking it before the skies blackened and it began to rain. Dragging herself to her feet, Minta went into the café to pay, the staff and a few customers looking at her as if she was mad. Her grazed knees had stiffened while she'd been sitting so still, and it hurt to move. There didn't seem to be any free taxis and she had to walk all the way back to the house in the rain, her hair sticking to her head. There was nowhere else to go, only there.

When she got in, she went straight upstairs to the bedroom and stared at herself in the mirror. Her hair, darkened by the rain, hung in rat's-tails about her head. There were dusty shadows around her eyes and her face looked dead, lifeless. Minta's heart filled with misery. She remembered Delia Nelson's tall, slim beauty and realised that the other girl had been right—how could Dane possibly prefer her? When he had made love to her had he closed his eyes, trying to pretend that she was Delia?

Dragging off her clothes, Minta dropped them on to the floor and put on a nightdress, then climbed into bed, regardless of her wet hair. She lay still, staring at the ceiling, not even trying to sleep. She felt completely punchdrunk, as if someone had knocked her into a state of semi-consciousness and her brain wouldn't work. Tomorrow. Tomorrow she would decide what to do. Now all she wanted was just to lie there, numbly cocooned in the warm bedcovers like a chrysalis, not having to think or feel, to put off living until tomorrow.

Dane came home at his usual time and came straight up to the bedroom when he didn't find her downstairs. 'Darling, what is it?' His face and voice were full of concern,

Minta stared into his face, searching for some sign of the truth, a touch of coldness in his eyes or tone, however slight, that would tell her he was putting on an act. But there was only what you would expect to find in the face of a man who came home and found his wife apparently unwell.

'It—it's nothing.' She turned her head away, unable to bear looking at him. 'I fell over, that's all. So I thought I'd rest for a while.'

'You fell?' he exclaimed sharply. 'Did you hurt yourself? My God, you're not having a miscarriage?'

There was real worry in his voice now, genuine fear; but not for her, only for his plans, she thought bitterly. Slowly she turned to look up at him. 'You wouldn't like that, would you?' she asked tonelessly.

'Like it? What the hell kind of a question is that?' His face went white. 'Are you trying to tell me . . .'

His hands went to the covers to jerk them back, but Minta shouted, 'No!' and grabbed the duvet. 'No, I'm not. Please, Dane, I just want to rest.'

He stared at her and put a hand on her head. 'Your hair is soaking! For God's sake, Minta, tell me what happened. Did you hurt yourself or not?'

'No, only my knees. I tripped over a broken paving stone, that's all,' she answered fretfully, wishing he would leave her alone.

'Show me.' This time he had his way and pulled back the covers, then lifted her nightdress so that he could see her knees. 'You haven't even cleaned them up! Why, darling? Please tell me what's the matter.' He sat on the edge of the bed and took her hand, looking at her with worried, anxious eyes.

Minta felt as if her heart was being torn out. If only she could believe that he really cared, that the worry was really for her alone. She wanted to reach out to him, beg him to hold her, tell him of all her doubts and fears and hear him laugh them away as figments of her imagination, or as the jealous spite of a rejected lover. But she only said, 'I felt dizzy after I fell over. I couldn't get a taxi and it started to rain.'

'Oh, my poor love!' His hand gripped hers as if trying to give her some of his strength, then he got up and went to the bathroom, coming back with a bowl of warm water. His touch incredibly gentle, he cleaned up her knees and then dried her hair with a towel, afterwards brushing it gently smooth again. Minta was too choked up to speak, too near to tears. If only this was true, if his concern were real! He was being so loving, so wonderful. For several minutes he held her in his arms, her head against his shoulder, gently stroking her hair. 'Are you hungry? Shall I get you something to eat?' he asked, but Minta only moved her head in refusal. 'Okay. Just lie down and I'll go and make you a hot drink.' He laid her gently back against the pillows, then bent to kiss her cold lips. Minta closed her eyes, willing herself not to respond, unable to trust her own instinct any more.

Dane straightened up and she heard him leave and go downstairs. She kept her eyes closed, trying to forget the worry in his face and the way he was looking after her, but knowing that she would remember it all her life. About ten minutes later he came back with a beaker of hot milk that tasted as if he'd added something stronger. He helped her to sit up, treating her like a child, talking to her reassuringly but not expecting an answer. He would make a wonderful father—the thought came unbidden into her mind and made Minta choke over her drink.

'Darling, are you all right?'

'Yes,' she nodded. 'It just—went down the wrong way.' She looked away, afraid he would see the wretchedness in her eyes.

Before she had finished the milk the doorbell rang and Dane went to answer it, coming back with a short, plump Spaniard whom he introduced as a doctor. It seemed that Dane had sent for him while he was making her drink. The doctor examined her carefully, asking questions in his heavily-accented English. Sometimes she didn't perfectly understand and Dane had to translate. Minta wished he wasn't there; she didn't want to answer questions about her body when he could hear. Not now. At last the doctor finished and the two men left her alone. She could hear them talking outside on the landing, and felt a burning resentment that the doctor could discuss her with Dane as if she had no rights over her own body. But maybe they still regarded a wife as just another of the man's possessions in the Canary Islands.

'He thinks you're fine,' Dane assured her when he rejoined her a few minutes later. 'But you're to take it easy for a couple of days and then go and see him again some time after Christmas.' He grinned, 'And he thinks you'll have a very beautiful baby—and wishes us lots, lots more. A man after my own heart!'

'I'm tired,' Minta turned her head away abruptly. 'I'd like to go to sleep now.'

'Of course.' She felt him looking down at her, then his lips touched her cheek, rested there for a moment. 'Goodnight, my love.'

Minta's hands clenched together under the covers and she had to bite her tongue to stop herself crying out in anguish. But then he was gone and she was alone with her unhappiness at last.

That night, Dane slept in the spare bedroom, and the next morning, when he looked in, Minta pretended to be asleep; after a moment's hesitation, he went out again. He had an important appointment that day which he couldn't miss, so she knew he had no choice but to leave her on her own. She didn't think he'd bother to come up again, but he did, taking her by surprise and catching her awake.

'Hi.' He smiled and bent to kiss her. 'How are you feeling this morning?'

'Much better, thank you.' Minta tried to avoid his eyes which were studying her face intently.

'Good. What would you like for breakfast?'

'Nothing.' She saw him start to open his mouth in protest and added quickly, 'At least, not right now. I think I'll just laze in bed for a while and get up and make myself something later on.'

'You'll stay in bed all day,' Dane told her firmly. 'Doctor's orders.'

'Oh, but . . .'

'No buts.' He put a finger against her lips. 'I've arranged for the woman who cleans the office to come on here later this morning. She'll do any cleaning that's necessary and prepare a meal for you. Her name's Señora Rodriguez. And she's agreed to come for the rest of the week. Then it will be Christmas and I'll take the week off and be able to look after you myself. So promise me that you'll rest today. Okay?'

'Okay,' Minta nodded, her voice husky.

'I wish I could stay with you today,' he said, 'but there's no way I can get out of that appointment with the planning department. If I put it off heaven knows when I'll be able to arrange it again. Sorry, darling. But we'll have all Christmas together.' Minta didn't answer, and he lifted a hand to gently stroke her cheek. 'I'm worried about you. I thought you were happy about the baby.'

'I—I am,' Minta muttered.

'Then perhaps it's your father who's on your mind. Have you heard from him?'

'No.' She shook her head.

'Well, maybe now's the time to make it up with him. It's Christmas, after all—and he'd want to know about the baby.' He glanced at his watch. 'But this is hardly the time to discuss it. Think about it and we'll talk tonight. Have a good rest, darling.' He straightened up, tall and extremely handsome in his dark suit, then bent and put a hand on either side of her face. 'And always remember that I love you,' he said earnestly. His lips found hers, gentle yet insistent, provoking a response she didn't want to give. His kiss drove everything else from her mind, her senses reacting of their own volition. Her lips opened under his, returning his embrace with a fierce, utterly desperate passion, her arms going round his neck to cling to him with all her strength.

'Sweetheart!' Dane said hoarsely, when at last she let him go. He took her hand and held the palm against his mouth, kissing it. 'Oh, Minta, I love you so much,' he murmured, so intensely that she hardly heard him. 'Don't worry, you're going to be fine—you and the baby. Oh hell, I wish I didn't have to leave you. But I'll be back as soon as I can. Rest now, darling.' He bent and kissed her on the tip of her nose, her hand still in his. 'Goodbye.'

He looked at her expectantly and she managed to say, 'Goodbye, Dane,' but her hand jerked within his.

His brows drew into a frown and he seemed about to say something else, but then the clock in the hall downstairs began to chime the hour and he gave a reluctant shrug. 'See you this evening.' He raised his hand in salute and turned to run downstairs.

Minta gave a sob of relief, knowing that if he'd stayed any longer, if he'd kissed her again, she wouldn't have been able to hold out, she'd have had to tell him everything. Which could either be the best or the worst thing she ever did; only time would ever tell. But now she would never know because time had run out for her

and Dane. And she had been given so little with him
before it all went sour.

But now there was no time to dwell on that. She had
to hurry. Dane had said that this Senõra Rodriguez
would be coming later this morning, and she had to be
away from here by then. Quickly Minta got up and
dressed, then phoned for a taxi while she packed a
couple of suitcases with clothes and her most treasured
possessions, the while being reminded vividly of the way
she had packed to leave her father's house such short
months ago. And with what high hopes. But,
fortunately, there was no time to wallow in nostalgia.
The taxi driver was at the door and she gave him her
cases, then there was only one thing left to do. Taking
Delia Nelson's letter from her handbag, she propped it
up where Dane was sure to see it. No other explanation
was necessary. With a last, heartbreaking look at the
house where she had known such exquisite happiness,
Minta turned and ran to the taxi.

She directed him first to the bank where she closed
her account, and then on to the airport, booking a seat
on the next plane to England. But instead of taking the
plane, she waited until a crowd of incoming passengers
flew in and mingled with them, getting another taxi to
drive her back into central Las Palmas, and immediately
afterwards taking a third taxi to the port, from where
she caught the local jet-foil over to the neighbouring
island of Tenerife. Dane, she had reasoned, would
expect her to go back to England and wouldn't look for
her further than the airport. But there was no way she
was going to go running back to her father so that he
could say, 'I told you so'. She had messed up her own
life and somehow she would just have to try and
straighten it out. From here on she was on her own.

CHAPTER SEVEN

THE Christmas bells rang out joyfully across the island and Minta lay in her narrow, uncomfortable bed listening to them, her thoughts far away with the two people in the world that she loved. Would either of them be missing her? she wondered. It would be the first Christmas she had ever spent away from her father. Before they had always been together, either at home or, mostly when she had been younger, at a hotel. Perhaps he was with Maggie now. He might even have married her, if he was lonely. Minta hadn't written to him or even sent him a card, not him or any of her friends and relations, because the postmark would have given her away, but she tried now to send her loving wishes to him, hoping that somehow he would know. And Dane? Would he be thinking of her? If he was it could only be in furious anger, knowing that she had found out and all his plans had been thwarted. He was probably living in fear that his financial backing would now be withdrawn, just when he needed it most, was probably even planning how he could get out with as much as he could and leave others to carry the blame and responsibility, Minta thought cynically.

She was becoming increasingly cold and cynical lately. For three days, after she had found this tiny hotel room in Puerto de la Cruz, she had done nothing but cry, but then she had deliberately buried all emotions, preferring not to feel anything at all than to be always grieving for what was past. So she had covered her blotchy skin with make-up and gone out and got herself a job at a restaurant in one of the main streets of this popular tourist resort. With her qualifications she could have had her pick of places. And she was to start after Christmas, although she would rather have started now so that she had something else to think about other than being alone. Or almost alone. Her hand went to her stomach. If anything happened to the baby she didn't think she'd be able to go on. That was all she had to live for now. The bells rang out again to signal the end of Christmas Mass, and Minta turned her head into the pillow, trying to shut them out.

'Ven are you going to stop saying no and come out vith me?' the young German who prepared the vegetables and salads demanded in his guttural accent.

'When are you going to take no for an answer and stop asking me?' Minta returned with more than a little annoyance in her tone. 'I don't want to go out with you, Klaus.' She lifted a tired hand to push a lock of hair out of her eyes. It was two o'clock in the morning and she was longing to go home and go to bed.

'Vy not? Vy you not like me?' He was tall and fair, typically Teutonic, and had come to Tenerife to improve his Spanish so that he could get a job as a courier.

'I do like you. But I don't want to go out with you— you or anyone,' Minta told him exasperatedly. She finished putting the last of the unused food away, then cleaned down her working surfaces, straightening up with a sigh, her back aching.

'I valk you to your hotel,' Klaus offered, unputdown-able.

'No!' She rounded on him fiercely. 'Just leave me alone, will you? Or I'll complain to the manager.'

That, at last, had some effect, and he turned sulkily away, leaving Minta free to change from her overall into a skirt and sweater and walk home alone through the virtually deserted streets. It was late February and the resort was filling up with winter break holiday-makers, gradually building up for the summer, but they were mostly older people and the place quietened down by two. Minta hated to think what it would be like in the summer when the restaurant stayed open even later. It was a fairly modern town in the north of the island, built up, as so many resorts were, from a little fishing village when tourists started to discover it. Now it was mostly hotels and arcades full of souvenir shops, bars and restaurants, catering solely for the tourists, but at least there was the Botanical Garden to walk in and the Lido where she could go to swim and sunbathe on her days off. The beaches were pretty hopeless as they were of black, volcanic pebbles and rock. Not that Minta bothered much; she had suffered from morning sickness in the first few weeks and it had pulled her down, making her want to rest whenever she could. But fortunately she seemed to be over that now.

Reaching her hotel, she said goodnight to the old man reading his paper in the lobby and went up to her room. It was a place frequented by students who had little money and he was used to people coming in late from their jobs. Minta undressed, washed, and climbed into bed, grateful for the exhaustion that sent her almost instantly to sleep, giving her only a few moments to think of Dane, to wonder where he was, and what he was doing. And who with? that cynical voice prompted, more and more often now.

Someone at the hotel had left behind the local English language newspaper. Minta read it over her coffee and croissants the next morning. It dealt mainly with Tenerife, with lots of adverts for the various tourist attractions, but in this edition there was an article about the annual carnival in Las Palmas in Gran Canaria. It lasted for two weeks and ended with a big parade through the streets, finishing up in the square of Parque Santa Catalina where she and Dane had often gone to sit and watch the world go by. She pushed the paper aside, but the advert haunted her. Dane had described the festival to her, telling her how everyone, young and old, dressed up in fancy costume and masks, parading round the town throughout the whole festival, about the rival bands who took it in turns to march round the town every evening, gathering a trail of people behind them. And next weekend she had two days off, two days which coincided with the end of the carnival.

The thought stayed with her all that week. Minta tried to concentrate on her work, which she greatly enjoyed except for the long hours. During the weeks she had been there, the manager had let her change and improve some of the menu and the clientele had already started to increase. They had even started to get some local inhabitants as well as tourists. And she had had a rise in pay which she was carefully saving along with the capital she had brought with her, in the meantime living very frugally, because she was going to need every penny she could get when she was no longer able to work and the baby came along. How she was going to manage then, Minta wasn't sure, but she had an idea for getting her own small flat and doing outside catering for some of the cafés in the town: cakes and

pastries, that kind of thing. That way she could look
after the baby at home without having to farm it out to
a nursery. But she knew that somehow she would cope,
which gave an indication of how she had learnt to stand
on her own two feet during the last couple of months.

But there was no use trying to pretend that she didn't
miss Dane. He was her first thought on waking and her
last at night. She missed him as sorely as a woman
misses a husband who has died. More perhaps, because
there was always the torment of wondering what he was
doing, whether he had gone after her to try and get her
back. Although she didn't think he would, not after
he'd seen that letter and talked to Delia Nelson. His
mistress. That part of it Minta tried not to think about,
because it was the hardest to bear, knowing that Dane
was still making love to Delia at the same time as her,
when she had thought everything was so perfect
between them. But being apart from him was like a
physical pain, always there, like a terminal illness from
which she would never recover, she thought with bitter
irony.

By the end of the week Minta had pushed the idea of
the festival right out of her mind, but somehow, when
she woke late on the Saturday, she found herself
stuffing a toothbrush into her pocket and using some of
her precious savings to pay for the jet-foil back to Las
Palmas, the big machine, half boat/half plane, rising up
on its huge hydrofoils and carrying them skimming over
the waves, unbelievably quickly.

There were quite a few people going back on the jet-
foil from a day trip to Tenerife and Minta was careful
to keep among them when they landed. She headed for
the big store, El Corte Inglés, and up to the third floor
where the fancy dress costumes were being sold, her

eyes continuously on the look-out for anyone who might recognise her. Although it was so late in the festival they still had lots of things on display: masks and wigs, grotesque gloves like monsters' hands as well as clothes. Minta had deliberately worn black slacks, a dark sweater and a loose black jacket, and now she picked out a wig of bright ginger, curly synthetic hair and one of those false shirt fronts that Victorian gentlemen used to wear. The wig made her look quite different and the false front hid her chest so that she looked like a boy. Then she added a doleful clown's mask to hide her face. No one would recognise her now and with any luck no one would even take her for a woman.

It was getting into the evening and already there were lots of people in costume thronging the streets, especially children, so Minta, although she felt ridiculous, wasn't at all out of place. She went first to Dane's office, hurrying past the traffic-laden roads, trying to ignore people who laughed at her costume and a drunk who wanted her to drink with him. But she had listened to the voluble people working in the restaurant kitchens and could tell him to go to hell in Spanish now. When she reached the office building she stood in a doorway opposite, looking up at Dane's window, but it seemed deserted. She waited until it was dusk and when no lights went on, knew that he wasn't there. She hadn't really expected him to be on a Saturday, but there had been just a chance, and it was so much easier to look for him there.

Retracing her steps, Minta walked the couple of miles to the house. It seemed a long way, although she had often walked it before and thought nothing of it, but she was hurrying and had a stitch in her side by the time she got there. She couldn't see any lights on in the upper storey at the front of the house but she couldn't see the ground floor because of the wall. For a quarter of an hour or so she hung around uncertainly, then nerved herself to go and peer through a crack in the gate. There was a light in the sitting-room. He was at home!

Minta stood there numbly, remembering the room and the improvements she had made to it with such loving attention. Was he there alone—or did he have that woman with him? Turning away, she found herself a seat on the low wall of a garden a little way down the road on the opposite side, a place where she could rest and watch the gate of Dane's house. She took off the mask, finding it hot and uncomfortable to wear for any length of time, and settled down to wait again, hoping against hope that he would come out and she would be able to see him.

She waited for almost two hours, gradually growing stiff and cold, glad of her sweater and jacket against the chill breeze in the air. Almost, she had become reconciled to the fact that he was going to stay in that evening and she wouldn't be able to see him after all, but she was quite prepared to go on waiting, all night if need be. But then, at almost nine o'clock, the gate swung open and he came out. Half asleep, Minta nearly missed him, but the clang of the gate—such a familiar sound—brought her back to reality with a jerk. Dane had come out and he was on foot, walking down the road towards her. And he was alone! All along she had been petrified that she would see him with Delia Nelson, but at least it would have proved that she had been right to leave him.

Hopping over the wall, Minta hid behind a hibiscus

bush until he had passed, then put on her mask again and began to follow him, still keeping to the opposite side of the street. He walked quite briskly so that Minta had to hurry to keep him in sight, heading back towards the centre of town where there were more people. As the pavements filled she had to move closer so that she wouldn't lose him in the crowd. It was quite dark now and she could see him outlined against the lights from shop windows and in the glow of the street lamps. Once he stopped at an intersection and, turning to see if there was any traffic coming, caught sight of her behind him. Minta froze, but he merely gave a small, amused smile at her costume and turned to walk on.

Somehow she forced her legs to work again and tottered after him. He reached a restaurant and went inside, glancing over his shoulder as he did so. The place was strange to Minta; she had never been there with him. Was he dining there alone, or was he meeting someone? Sidling up to the window, she peered inside. Dane had been shown to a table not far away and was sitting facing the window. Again he was alone. She went to move away, but then stopped as a waiter came up to him and he looked up, the light falling fully on his face. For a moment he looked like a stranger; his face was thinner than she remembered, with a drawn, haggard look about his features. His mouth was set into a hard line and there was bleakness in his eyes. He looked like a man who was suffering great unhappiness. Surprise held Minta as she stared at him, wondering what could have made him change so much; only the failure of his business, she surmised and wondered how it could have come about. Or maybe Delia Nelson had left him and everything he had done had been in vain.

Some children noticed her clown's face staring in the window, and pointed her out to their parents, making Dane look in her direction. Hastily Minta moved away. It looked as if he would be in the restaurant for some time, so she bought a hamburger from a stall and stood in the darkness of a recessed shop doorway near the restaurant, where she could watch the entrance. A couple of seamen from one of the merchant ships in the port walked by, saw her and stopped to chat her up. Minta tried to ignore them, but they were persistent, crowding her into the doorway and trying to put their hands on her. She was afraid at first, but then it began to dawn on her that they thought she was a boy, so she swiftly made it plain to them that she wasn't, and they roared with laughter and went on their way. But she would have to be careful; they could quite easily have turned nasty.

It was eleven before Dane left the restaurant. He stood in the doorway for a couple of minutes, looking around him as if making up his mind which way to go, then he turned to the right, making for the park which was the centre of the carnival celebrations. The square was absolutely crowded with people, nearly all of them in some sort of fancy dress. Even some of the tourists were wearing funny hats and masks. In the centre of the square was a raised stage where a band of men all dressed as Roman soldiers were playing, surrounded by costumed people who danced or stood around and clapped and sang to the music.

Because of the crowds, Minta had to move to within only a few yards of Dane, but he was moving only slowly through the throng and she didn't have too much difficulty. He stood on the edge of the crowd around the bandstand for a short while, then moved across to sit at a vacant table outside one of the cafés. Minta stood hesitantly in the deep shadow of a tree trunk for a while and then, the success of her disguise giving her confidence, did the same. Her feet ached and she was dying for a cup of coffee, the smell of which had drifted to her on the breeze.

They sat only a few tables apart, Minta trying not to make it too obvious that she was watching him, but her eyes, behind the sad clown's face, going often towards Dane, unable to keep away. Seeing him again had brought all the old emotions flooding back: love, need, desire. It had been so long since he had last held her in his arms and told her he loved her. So long since they had made love. Her body ached for him. Minta picked up her cup of coffee, lifting the mask a little so that she could drink its bitter hotness. Looking up, she was shocked to find Dane apparently watching her, but his eyes moved on, resting on someone else in carnival costume, and she breathed again. She shouldn't have come. It had been a stupid, masochistic thing to do. It had brought back all the torments that she had tried so hard to smother in the last two months. She would drink this and then go, make a vow with herself never to be so stupid again.

She raised her cup—and suddenly felt her left wrist taken in a vicelike grip. With a gasp of surprise, she looked up and saw Dane staring down at her hand. Her eyes followed his. Her rings! God, she'd forgotten to take off her rings and he'd recognised them! Her horrified eyes rose to meet his. Dane, too, seemed unable to believe the evidence of his own eyes. But then he gave a strangled sound and reached up to tear the mask from her face, snapping the elastic and throwing it onto the ground.

'Minta!'

The name came out as a gasping cry. Dane was staring into her face, his own white with shock in the lamplight.

Her surprise at being discovered somewhat less than Dane's at finding her, Minta recovered more quickly and reacted quite instinctively, throwing the cup she was holding and its contents into his face. He automatically recoiled and put up a hand to protect his eyes which gave Minta a chance to pull her wrist free from his hold. Desperately wiping some of the coffee from his eyes, Dane reached for her again, but she overturned the table so that he stumbled over it. Then Minta turned and ran, diving into the darkness of the trees, dodging through the crowds, and jumping over the low fences round the flower beds, in a mad panic in case he caught her. She pushed and battled her way out of the square, bumping into a mob of people who were following a new band in her mad haste, once almost being knocked down by a man who got annoyed when she cannoned into him. But she somehow managed to keep her balance and bolted out of the square, running up one of the main roads leading back into the centre of town. The street was still crowded, but it had been closed to traffic because of the carnival, so she was able to run up the centre of the road, her feet flying as if the devil was after her. And he was. When she reached the corner, Minta glanced back—and gave a cry of horror as she saw Dane running up the road a couple of hundred yards behind her.

Too late she realised that the brightly coloured wig must have given her away, acting like a beacon for him to follow. As soon as she rounded the corner, she tore it from her head and threw it into an open doorway, her hair tumbling loose on her shoulders, then she ran on, heading for the back streets where there were dark alleys and places where she could hide. But he must have guessed her intention, because she could hear him pelting after her. The silly plastic shirt-front came loose and flapped in front of her face, so she tore it off and threw it aside, her breath coming in ragged gasps now. She reached the next corner, went on for only a few yards, then plunged down a narrow lane between older houses, came out into a small square and ran down one of several alleys that gave off it, her footsteps and loud, panting breaths echoing against the walls. At the other end she paused for a moment to get her breath, hardly able to see. The stitch in her side had come back, tearing at her with every step she took, and she knew she couldn't keep going much longer. Then the brightly lit sign of a disco swam into focus not far down the road and she ran towards it, giving a last look back to make sure Dane wasn't in sight before plunging into the doorway.

The place was full of young people, most of them in grotesque carnival costumes, reminding her momentarily of the club she had gone to in London on the first night she had met Dane. It was full of smoke which hung on the still, hot air and lit only by flashing psychedelic lights which battered the eyes as the loud irregular beat of the music battered the ears. Minta pushed her way deep into the back of the room like a thief trying to hide in a crowd. But then she saw a door with the universal sign of a little man and woman over it and went through, with some vague idea of locking herself in the ladies' loo. Luck, however, was with her, because at the end of the corridor leading past the loos there was another door which, when she tried it, opened into a yard at the back of the disco. Cautiously she went through. The yard was surrounded on all sides by a high wall, but she managed to stack up some boxes and climbed it, dropping to the ground on the other side with a thump that knocked the wind out of her.

Staggering to her feet, Minta hurried on, forever looking back over her shoulder in case Dane should happen to find her. Only when she had covered a couple of miles and knew for sure that Dane wasn't following her did she start to relax a little. By now she was completely exhausted and gratefully lay down on a bench in a small park to rest. She had no real idea where she was, but guessed that she was near the old town and the cathedral; not that it really mattered; in Las Palmas you were never far from the sea, and once it was light and she knew in which direction it lay, she would easily be able to get her bearings. Pulling her jacket more tightly around her, she prepared to settle down for the night, giving up her earlier intention of finding a small hotel in which to spend the night. Now all she wanted to do was get off this island as soon as possible and back to the safety of Tenerife.

Sometimes she dozed a little, but mostly lay awake, thinking of Dane, of how he had looked—and wondering why. At first light she washed her face in a nearby fountain, her body stiff and cramped from the hard bench. There were few people about as Minta made her way back to the jet-foil. The first one left at eight, so she had a long time to wait, but at least she would be sure of getting a seat; it often got quite full of holidaymakers going to spend the day on the other island. Eight came at last and Minta hurried on board, grateful to have an end to her stupid escapade.

CHAPTER EIGHT

SHE should never have gone back. Life resumed on
Tenerife much as before, but now Minta felt completely
unsettled again, and it was hard to take. Never having
done a full-time job before, she found the long hours
and hard work were beginning to tell on her and she
lost weight, which ordinarily wouldn't have done her
any harm but was all wrong now. In some ways, of
course, it was fortunate, because no one at the
restaurant or the hotel suspected she was pregnant. She
wanted to hang on to both her room and her job as
long as possible. But the cooking, too, started to
become repetitious, the manager refusing to vary the
menu from week to week as Minta wanted, saying that
the tourists would only order dishes they recognised.
Depression and tiredness settled on her like a black
cloak, and she would gladly have gone to bed and just
stayed there.

But thinking about the baby helped, and gradually,
over the next two or three weeks, Minta managed to
take hold of life again. She bought some wool and
needles, and although she hadn't done any knitting
since she was at school, determinedly set about making
the baby a little coat, although she seemed to spend
quite a time unpicking the thing. One morning, she sat
in her room, wrestling with the knitting pattern and
deciding that she would have to give birth to a giant if
this was going to fit. She sighed, realising that she was
going to have to unpick it and start again; she must

have gone fundamentally wrong somewhere. At this rate her poor baby would have to go around naked! There was a knock on her door and she thankfully put the knitting aside, tucking the pattern out of sight, knowing that it was Beatriz, one of the hotel maids, who always came to change the sheets and towels at this time on Wednesdays and usually stayed to have a chat, their conversation a mixture of broken English and Spanish.

Pulling the door wide, she said, 'Come in, Beatriz. I . . .' then stopped dead.

She ought to have known that Dane would find her. That having seen her again he wouldn't give up until he tracked her down. He stood in the doorway, his face set into a grim mask, his grey eyes ice-cold and menacing.

Without thinking, Minta immediately tried to shut the door against him, but he kicked it open with his foot, knocking it out of her hands and sending it crashing back on its hinges. Then he strode into the room and slammed the door, shutting her in with him in a room that suddenly seemed as small as a cupboard.

They stood staring at each other, Minta too stunned and afraid to speak, Dane too angry. His eyes were on her face, devouring it, and it seemed to cost him a great effort before he ordered, through gritted teeth, 'Get your things together. I'm taking you back with me.'

'No!' Minta backed away from him. 'I won't go with you!'

'You'll come. You'll come if I have to drag you.' He glared at her, his jaw thrust forward threateningly.

'No, I won't. Get out of here! You have no right to . . .'

'No right?' He strode furiously towards her and pushed her roughly back against the wall when she tried to move away. 'I have a perfect right to do anything I damn well want to you. Do you know how I've searched for you? *Do you?*' He gripped her arms. 'Why the hell did you run out on me?'

'You know why.' The old bitterness came flooding back as she finally accused him. 'You lied and cheated from the first day we met. You never loved me—it was always Delia Nelson. You kept on seeing her and making love to her even after I found out. All you ever wanted me for was to get financial security from my father. You just . . .'

'That isn't true! Not one word of it. For God's sake, why can't you believe me?'

'Believe you?' Minta laughed harshly. 'You must be joking! I proved that you lied. I phoned someone in my father's firm and he told me that you'd got the bank's backing. But you denied it, you said it was some syndicate.'

'Because I'd promised your father that I wouldn't tell you. He didn't want you to know.'

'Which suited you very well,' Minta retorted scornfully. 'You're a fool if you expect me to believe that. Why the hell wouldn't he want me to know?'

'Possibly because he's as stubborn as you are and didn't want you to know that he'd had to climb down. That he'd lost the battle. He was as jealous as hell of you marrying me—of you marrying any man, if it comes to that.'

'That's a perfectly idiotic thing to say!'

'Is it?' Dane asked jeeringly. 'The relationship you two had was closer than that of any other father and daughter I've ever known. When you turned up at my hotel room in London that night it was more in defiance of your father than because you wanted to go to bed with me.'

'That isn't true!' Minta's pale cheeks flushed red with anger. 'I was in love with you.'

'Love! What the hell do you know about love? Oh, you said it often enough, but you didn't have the least idea what it means. You're just a spoilt brat who's always been given everything you wanted. As soon as someone threw the slightest suspicion on me, you took off, convinced that I'm every kind of a scoundrel. And that after everything we had together,' he added with bitter revulsion.

'For God's sake!' Minta broke from his hold and turned to glare at him. 'Do you call confirmed lies and adultery suspicion? She told me! I went to see your damn mistress and she told me—how you'd used me, and even how you'd made her prostitute herself for you. And how you intended to get rid of me when the baby was born and you didn't need me any more.' Her voice rose hysterically. 'Do you really think I was going to hang around after that?'

Dane's face had gone very pale. He stood with his hands clenched at his sides, his mouth set into a thin, bitter line. 'You really believed that poison? She was a jealous, spiteful woman and you believed her?' He shook his head as if to clear it. 'Even that she'd prostituted herself for me? Okay, she went to bed with the owner of that land, but because she wanted to, because she's that kind of woman. But if you believed her then that proves you never really loved me. If you had you'd have trusted me, no matter what she'd said. You would at least have faced me with it instead of running off and letting me go through hell trying to find you. Not knowing where you were or what had happened to you.' Painfully he added, 'It must take some special form of sadism to inflict that kind of cruelty on anyone!'

Minta bit her lip. True or false? Always the same question. He would behave the same either way, say the same words. And nothing had changed. Even though she still loved him she couldn't give him the benefit of the doubt, not when she had so much at stake. 'Why shouldn't I believe her? She knew everything about me: that I was pregnant, that I couldn't swim very well, about my father backing you; only you could have told her those things—and after you said that you'd never see her again.'

'I admit I told Delia that I'd got financial backing from your father's bank when we first came to the Canaries. But as I never expected her to meet you it hardly seemed to matter that she knew. I certainly never expected her to use it as a weapon against us,' Dane exclaimed bitterly. 'As for your swimming—she came to our hotel soon after we arrived here; to get a look at you, I suppose. I saw her up at the pool one day—and had the hell of a row with her about it afterwards.'

'And the baby? How are you going to explain away the fact that she knew about that?' Minta asked sarcastically.

He shrugged. 'I can't. I certainly never told her. Maybe she guessed when she saw you.'

'You make it sound so plausible.' Dane looked up quickly at that, a speculative light in his eyes. 'But then liars always do,' she added with relentless punishment.

'What the hell do I have to do to convince you?' he demanded grimly.

'Nothing. There's nothing you can say or do that will ever make me change my mind. The fact still remains that you're completely dependent on my father's backing. And for that you need me—or my child. And if you lay a hand on me again, I'll scream the place down!' Her voice rose in alarm as he took an angry stride towards her.

'Don't worry,' he sneered, his voice ice-cold. 'I have no desire to touch you. And for your information, I no longer have the backing of your father's bank. I don't need it. My brother died last month, of natural causes, as it happens, and it seemed that he had taken out a big insurance policy when he was flush some years ago. It was enough to clear the rest of his debts that I've been struggling to pay off and to make me independent, especially as the time-share project has really taken off and is starting to show a profit.'

Minta stared at him, then said dully, 'I don't believe you.'

His mouth twisted in disgust. 'Somehow I thought you'd say that! Well, believe it or not, that's up to you. It makes no difference; I'm still taking you back home with me. So start packing.'

'Like hell I will!' Minta snapped back. 'If you don't need my father's money, then you don't need me. Or have you forgotten that?' she demanded with mock sweetness.

'I don't have to remember because it never came into it. I'm taking you back because you're going to have my child. When it's born we can work things out, but until then you're going to live with me and be taken care of, whether you like it or not. It's my kid and I'm not going to let you endanger it because of your stupid pride and blindness. Besides,' he added scornfully, 'a child needs love, and you can't even recognise it, let alone give it!'

Minta glared at him, that last knife thrust hurting more than he could possibly have guessed. If he'd loved her he would have known how much she cared, that she had only left him because she loved him so much. And she still didn't know whether to believe him; he could be making up the story about the insurance policy just to get her to go back with him. Cold anger filled her, and a desire to hit back and hurt as he had hurt her. 'You're wasting your time,' she said shortly. 'There isn't going to be any baby.'

He stared at her. 'What do you mean?'

'You heard me,' she jeered. 'Do you really think that I'd go through with having your child after what you did to me? *No way.* I got rid of it. I had an abortion. Now do you understand? There isn't going to be any baby!'

Dane stood as if turned to stone, completely frozen, his eyes staring into her face. Then, after what seemed an eternity, his eyes travelled slowly down her body, seeing her thinness, her prominent hipbones emphasising the flatness of her stomach. 'You bitch!' He spat the words at her in a groan of mingled pain, anger and despair. 'Oh, God—you cruel, sadistic little bitch!' Then he started towards her, with such a look of rage on his face that Minta instinctively backed quickly away, but she stumbled against a small table that came down, with its contents, on top of her.

Minta gave a cry of fear as she fell and then lay still, too scared to move. Dane picked up the table and threw it across the room, then stood over her, his face murderous. In that moment Minta thought that she was going to die, that he would kill her. He loomed over her, his fists clenched, white and trembling with rage. But then his face twisted in pain and tears came into his eyes. Turning abruptly on his heel, he strode out of the room, slamming the door behind him.

Slowly Minta sat up, staring at the closed door. She

didn't attempt to stand or start clearing up the mess, she just sat there, gazing at the door for a very long time.

She didn't go to work that day, phoning the restaurant to say that she was sick, and that evening she had her second visitor. This time it wasn't entirely unexpected, but even so, when she opened the door and saw her father standing there, she could only stand dumbly, not knowing what to say. Then, whether it had been his intention or not, he stepped into the room, took her in his arms and held her for a long, wordless moment.

'How did you find me?' Minta asked at last. 'Did Dane tell you?'

'Yes, he phoned me this morning and more or less ordered me to come and get you. I caught the first plane.' He held her away from him. 'My dear child, what on earth's been happening to you?'

She tried to smile. 'Nothing much. Everything.' Suddenly the tears were running down her cheeks. 'Oh, Daddy, I've been such a fool!'

'Come on, you'd better tell me all about it.' He sat her down beside him on the edge of the bed, his arm round her, and listened as she poured it all out, all her doubts and suspicions, how she had left Dane, everything—except the one big lie she had told Dane at the end.

'Yes, you have been a fool,' Richard Tennant agreed when she had finished. 'Most of all in coming to live here instead of coming home to me. But you always were as stubborn as a mule. Did you really think I wouldn't take you in?'

'You didn't write to me or try to get in touch, not once,' Minta pointed out.

'No—well, I admit I was more than a little angry, and I decided to let you make the first move. Pride, I suppose. But surely you knew that you could always come back and that I'd give you whatever help I could?'

Minta stood up and moved across the room; she had tidied it again and there was no sign of Dane's fury except for a broken glass in the wastepaperbasket. 'It really doesn't matter now, does it? It's too late.'

Her father looked at her narrowly. 'Dane said it was all over between you. Is that true?'

She shrugged. 'What else did he say?'

'Not a great deal. He said most of it when he came over to England just before Christmas, looking for you. He was convinced that you'd come back to me. He said then that you'd had a misunderstanding and you'd walked out. It threw him completely when he found you weren't with me. It threw me, too, if it comes to that.' He added grimly, 'We've both been frantic with worry about you.'

'I'm sorry,' Minta said inadequately. 'But I had to get away, and I didn't think you wanted me.' She looked down at her hands. 'Did he tell you I was pregnant?'

'Yes. But from something he said this morning, I gather that's no longer the case?'

Minta didn't deny or confirm it, instead asking, 'Did you know that his brother had died?'

'Yes, it was in the papers. And a couple of weeks later I received a letter from Dane saying that he no longer needed my bank's backing. A very curt letter, I might add. So it seems he managed to salvage something from the wreck of his brother's estate.

'So that at least was true,' Minta murmured to herself.

But her father heard her. 'I imagine that most of

what he told you was true. I was dead against your marrying him because you'd known him such a short time and because he was stuck with trying to pay off his brother's debts. Not that he need have done, but it seemed a point of honour with him. And I was afraid that the gambling streak might have rubbed off on him, although I was completely wrong about that. And again, time-share projects are always a risky business until enough people start to buy. Everything seemed to be against him; I was sure he'd go under. Maybe I even wanted him to go under,' he admitted ruefully. 'I certainly didn't want him to take you away.'

'Did you make him promise not to tell me that you'd let the bank back him?'

'Yes.' He frowned. 'Maybe it would have been better if I hadn't made it a condition that he wouldn't tell you.'

'Yes,' Minta agreed unsteadily, turning away. 'Maybe it would.'

'Well, that's all water under the bridge. We'll go back to England and you can get a divorce, put all this behind you. Maybe in time you'll be able to forget it ever happened.' He looked at her hopefully, but Minta still stood with her back to him, gazing out of the window at the sky turning to dusk. 'Let me help you pack,' he offered. 'I've checked and there's a plane leaving for England later tonight. We could be at home by the morning.'

She turned then, but he had a feeling that she hadn't been listening to him. 'I'm sorry, Daddy, but I'm not going back with you, not tonight at any rate. I have to see Dane once more and ask him to take me back.'

'He said everything was finished, that the marriage was over.'

'Yes, I know. But that was because I lied to him about the baby. It made him—angry.'

'I imagine it might have,' Richard Tennant agreed wryly. 'I take it you're still going to have it?'

'Yes.'

'My dear girl, what a hopeless mess you've got yourself into! Are you quite sure this is what you want? It's possible that Dane might react violently, you know.'

'That's a risk I'll have to take,' she replied steadily.

He looked at her for a long moment, then nodded. 'All right, I'll help you all I can. What would you like me to do?'

Putting a hand on his arm, Minta smiled up at him. 'Thank you. But you don't have to if you'd rather not. I can manage alone, you know.'

'So it seems. You've grown up, haven't you? You're not my little girl any more. Well,' he sighed rather sadly, 'I suppose I had to face up to it one day. But I'll still help, I *want* to. I'm afraid I'm more than a little to blame for what's happened to you.'

'Then will you help me to get to Gran Canaria?'

'Now? Tonight?'

'Yes, it has to be tonight.'

'All right, we'll see what we can do. You'd better start packing.'

The last jet-foil had already left, but in the end they managed to get a passage on a small ferry-boat that was taking some workers across from one island to the other, arriving at Gran Canaria at about ten o'clock. Then they took a taxi to the house.

Minta didn't get out at once. They sat looking out at the quiet, tree-lined street. 'Are you going to marry Maggie?' she asked at length.

'Maggie?' He laughed. 'Now can you see Maggie marrying a grandfather?' Then, after a moment, 'I don't know. We got pretty close after you left. Maybe. I admit I thought about it.'

'Good.' She reached out and took his hand. 'Marriage can be a pretty wonderful thing, can't it? When you get it right. Thank you for coming to find me. It means a great deal to me.'

'My dear girl!' He held her for a minute and kissed her on the forehead. 'Good luck. I'll be out here, waiting.'

'Only for ten minutes. Then you must go or you'll miss your plane. It calls here after Tenerife.'

'Promise me you'll come home if it doesn't go well,' he said anxiously.

'I promise. Tomorrow. Or I'll phone you. Goodbye, Daddy.'

They clasped hands again and then Minta got out of the taxi, stood for a minute looking at the house, then squared her shoulders and walked determinedly towards it.

She opened the gate and closed it quietly behind her, shutting out the outside world, the past, everything. There was a light shining out from the living-room and the curtains weren't drawn. Minta looked in and saw Dane sprawled in a chair, his jacket and tie off and his shirt undone. He had a glass in his hand. She used her key to unlock the front door and walked quietly into the room.

He had obviously been drinking for some time; there was a half empty decanter of whisky on the low table in front of him. He looked up when she walked in, but didn't jump or anything, just sat silently gazing at her through heavy-lidded eyes. 'You're real,' he said eventually.

'Yes.'

Dane motioned to the decanter. 'I'm drinking to forget you.'

'And have you?'

He gave a short, bitter laugh. 'Hell, no. How can I ever forget what you did to me? And I'm not drunk; I'm not even tight.' He put the glass on the table and pushed it away in disgust. 'What have you come back for? To put another knife in the wound?'

'No.'

'No,' he agreed bitterly. 'The wound's already mortal. So why? To collect the rest of your things? Go ahead; the sooner I see the last of you the better.'

'No, that wasn't why I came back. I wanted to see you.'

His jaw tightened and he reached out and filled his glass again, holding it so tightly that his knuckles showed white as he carried it to his mouth and emptied it. 'Okay, so now you've had your pound of flesh. Now get out of here.'

'Not yet. Not until I've said what I came to say.'

Dane looked at her with pain-filled eyes. 'For God's sake, Minta, get out of here. I can't take any more from you.'

Immediately she was on her knees beside him. 'Oh, Dane, I'm sorry—I'm so terribly sorry. I didn't know. Not until I saw your face when I told you about the baby. I didn't understand. And I was so afraid for the baby. I didn't know what to do. And it was all so perfect, I couldn't believe that it could be so perfect . . .' The words came tumbling out as she gazed up at him entreatingly.

'What the hell are you saying?' He caught hold of her shoulders and pushed her away from him.

'I'm trying to tell you that I'm sorry. That I want to—that I want to come back.'

He stared at her, then got angrily to his feet and strode across the room. 'Get out of here!' he shouted. 'Get out before I go mad! My God, do you think I can take any more of your games?'

'It isn't a game; I mean it. Dane, I love you.'

'You expect me to believe that?' He gave a shout of laughter.

Minta's face went white, but she said bravely, 'Why not? You expected me to believe you against all the odds.'

'But you didn't.' His lip curled derisively.

'I couldn't take the risk, not when I had the baby to consider. But I never stopped loving you. And I never will. I just couldn't go on living what I thought was a lie.'

His face bleak, Dane glared at her silently. From outside she heard the sound of a car starting up and driving away. Her father had given her far longer than the promised ten minutes.

Dane turned away. 'How can you talk about caring for the baby after what you did?'

'I can—make it up to you,' she said with difficulty.

He swung round to face her. 'Give me more babies, do you mean? Nothing could take that child's place. It was conceived in a love that was mutually perfect, in a physical expression of that love that was the most wonderful thing I'd ever known. Or so I thought,' he added bitterly.

'It could be again.' Minta put out a hand towards him, but he thrust it aside.

'Oh, sure,' he said derisively. 'And I'd have to live with the constant thought that if I got you pregnant and we had the slightest misunderstanding about something, you'd go right out and have another abortion. Well, no, thanks. That isn't something I want on my conscience.'

'Dane, please! Listen to me.' She put her hands on his arms appealingly. 'I—I lied to you. I wanted to hurt you and I said the first thing that came into my head. Do you understand? I didn't have an abortion. I'm still going to have the baby. All I ever wanted to do was to protect it—because it was yours. Because it was all I had left of you.' Her voice trailed away and she looked down, unable to meet his eyes.

Dane stood very still, so silent that she could hear his heart beating, then a violent tremor ran through his body; she could feel it under her hands.

'I know it was an unforgivable thing to do,' Minta said slowly, 'and I know I hurt you by walking out on you and not trusting you. I wanted to—oh, so much! You don't know what it was like; everything was against you and yet I couldn't stop loving you—didn't want to. But it was torture, like being torn apart. The weeks since I left you have been the worst I've ever known. I missed you so much. And I thought of you all the time, every day. My thoughts and my love were always yours. Always.' She lifted her head slowly to look at him, and found him gazing down at her intently, a new light in his eyes. 'That's why I came back at carnival time. I couldn't bear living without you. I wanted to see you again—just once.'

'Oh, dear God!' Dane lifted his hands, slowly unclenched his fists and put them on her shoulders, then moved them down her back, drawing her towards him until she was standing against him. They stood silently for a while, too overwhelmed by emotion to speak, until Dane said huskily, 'You put me through the worst kind of hell today. I thought I'd lost you, that you'd completely turned against me. I don't know where I was heading. I only know that I didn't care any more, that nothing mattered unless I had you.'

Her body trembling, Minta lifted tear-filled eyes to look into his. 'I know that saying sorry isn't enough, but I'll try and make it up to you, I swear I will. If—if you'll take me back.'

'Take you back? How can I—when you never left my heart?'

'Oh Dane!' She threw her arms round his neck and clung to him. 'I love you so much. Don't let me go—please don't ever let me go!'

His arms tightened round her, crushing her to him so that he hurt her, moulding her body into his. He gave a strange, strangled groan and wound his hand in her hair, pulling her head back so that he could gaze into her face. Quickly he bent and took her mouth, kissing her with a desperate need, in a kiss that wasn't sexual, but more a reassurance of her presence, a confirmation of the love that had flared the first time they'd met and never really died. Now it burnt again, perhaps more intensely, and both of them knew with that kiss that nothing would ever come between them again.

'I need you.' His lips moved down her throat, hot and insistent. 'God, how I need you!'

'I know—oh, I know. It's been so long.' Her fingers dug into his shoulders as she moved against him, wanting to be closer still.

Dane straightened up and looked at her, and now there was joy in his grey eyes. 'How long do we have—three months?'

Minta smiled. 'About that.'

'Then I think we'd better make the most of it, don't you? The two of us.'

'Until we become the three of us,' she agreed huskily.

Dane smiled back at her, then put an arm round her waist, reached up to turn off the light, and led her from the room.

Coming Next Month in Harlequin Presents!

735 THE GREAT ESCAPE Amanda Carpenter
Can an American heiress escape from her fortune? Not when she is pursued from Kentucky to Ohio by a private detective. But can she believe his claim that he has her best interests at heart?

736 ONCE A LOVER Claire Harrison
He is no longer her husband, her lover or her friend. But he has the crazy idea that he can miraculously alter the past and give them a future together—as husband and wife.

737 DAWN OF A NEW DAY Claudia Jameson
A young woman's vacation in the Bahamas seems like a dream come true until she finds herself having to share her seclusion with a man who thinks she—like most women—finds him irresistibly attractive.

738 WANTING Penny Jordan
An English model meets her match when she unwittingly challenges the master of the game to her favorite sport of enticement and denial. Winner takes all . . . and she forfeits her heart!

739 WORKING RELATIONSHIP Madeleine Ker
Her love affair with film almost ends in Tibet when a filmmaker works alongside her idol, a legendary director. He sets impossible standards for her as a professional—and as a woman.

740 A LOST LOVE Carole Mortimer
Her new face and new identity don't protect a desperate woman when she comes face-to-face and heart-to-heart with the one man who must never know that she is still alive—her husband.

741 RUN SO FAR Peggy Nicholson
A volunteer crisis-center worker loses her objectivity when her heart goes out to a man who is as much on the run as is his runaway son. The man is on the run from love!

742 ROUGH AND READY Elizabeth Oldfield
The life of a cashier in a fast Soho casino is no life for the respectable young widow of a policeman—according to the club's Welsh bodyguard. But why would a man like him even care?

Harlequin Celebrates Thirty-five Years of Excellence

---

6 TOP HARLEQUIN AUTHORS—6 CLASSIC BOOKS!

Join us in celebrating as we reissue six Harlequin novels by some of the best authors in series-romance-publishing history. These books still capture the delight and magic of love as much today as they did when they were originally published by Harlequin. The fact that they transcend time attests to their excellence.

THE 1950s
Nurse/Doctor books—
"delightful books with happy endings."

1. GENERAL DUTY NURSE
   by Lucy Agnes Hancock
2. HOSPITAL CORRIDORS
   by Mary Burchell

THE 1960s
An era of "armchair travel" and exotic settings for Harlequin readers

3. COURT OF THE VEILS
   by Violet Winspear

THE 1970s
Harlequin becomes a household word and introduces Harlequin Presents—today, still the most popular series of contemporary romance fiction

4. BAY OF NIGHTINGALES
   by Essie Summers
5. LEOPARD IN THE SNOW
   by Anne Mather

THE 1980s
World-renowned authors continue to ensure Harlequin's excellence in romance series publishing

6. DAKOTA DREAMIN'
   by Janet Dailey

RIDE A PAINTED PONY

by BEVERLY SOMMERS
The third
HARLEQUIN AMERICAN ROMANCE
PREMIER EDITION

A prestigious New York City publishing company decides to launch a new historical romance line, led by a woman who must first define what love means.